Ravenswood

Presented to

Benenden, UK

Global Exchange Programme
2012

Vicki Steer

_____Principal

Also by Kate Constable

Cicada Summer

Winter of Grace

Always Mackenzie

The Chanters of Tremaris series

The Singer of All Songs

The Waterless Sea

The Tenth Power

The Taste of Lightning

Crow Country

Kate Constable

ALLEN&UNWIN

First published in 2011

Allen & Unwin
83 Alexander Street
Crows Nest NSW 2065
Australia
Phone: (61 2) 8425 0100
Fax: (61 2) 9906 2218
Email: info@allenandunwin.com
Web: www.allenandunwin.com

A Cataloguing-in-Publication entry is available from the
National Library of Australia
www.trove.nla.gov.au

ISBN 978 1 74237 395 9

Cover and text design by Design by Committee
Crow and feathers illustration by Ngarra Murray
Set in 12/16 pt Baskerville by Midland Typesetters, Australia
This book was printed in April 2012 at McPhersons Printing Group
76 Nelson St, Maryborough Victoria 3465

10 9 8 7 6 5 4

*In memory of all the Jimmy Ravens
who fought and died for their country,
and who should not be forgotten.*

Foreword

A Crow's breath, a story and a girl's dream

Waa the Crow is in abundance in Boort, the home of the Yung Balug Clan. Waa is the commanding totem of the Dja Dja Wurrung, a wise but cheeky feathered One, a friend of the Dja Dja Wurrung since the Dreamtime, the shadow of our Ancestors' traditions and stories both past and future.

The town called Boort is a crow's breath northwest of Bendigo, three hours from the big smoke of Melbourne, two lakes, a creek and a hill.

Boort is Dja Dja Wurrung for 'smoke on the hill', messenger Country, Dja Dja Wurrung Country where Headmen sent intricate smoke signals to their Kulin neighbors as far away as Terrick Terrick and the Murray River. The past home of Girribong, Lerimburneen and Walpanumin, the headmen of the local Yung Bulag clan, Boort is now a typical Victorian country town overcoming their collective struggles to educate, feed and house their families.

We see the Headman's messages in the many hundreds of scarred trees, in the burial grounds, middens and mounds. We see the messages in Waa's mystical plaintive calls through the red gums and waterways, sending the messages of stories long past and into the journey of life. As the shiny feathered One says:

> *'This is a secret place, a story place.' The crow tilted its head, eyes black as jet beads. 'Crow's people came to this place. Now they are gone. The stories are always. Who tells Crow's stories now? Where are the dreams, when the dreamers are gone? Where are the stories, when no one remembers?'*

Every town and city has its dreamers and crow story, if only we all looked and understood the words of Waa.

Kate Constable has written a lively and highly commendable story, and most certainly the Yung Bulag Clans commend a good Australian story about Waa and Bunjil exploring, probing and informing our shared history and culture.

Waa and Sadie's story is about the justice of friendship, respect, reconciliation and recognition of People, land and culture. *Crow Country* is a spiritual cultural collaboration for all who love a good story.

Dja Dja Wurrung Yung Balug Clan,
Elder Gary Murray
Boort, June 2011

The crow wheeled high in the clear winter sky. The land was spread beneath, laid out like a map, like an open book. The lines of the creeks, and the bumps and sags of the hills and swamps held the stories of the country's ancient history, the marks of its creation.

Far below, the crow saw a tiny speck move along a muddy track. It was a human girl-child. She tramped along, her head down, ignoring the country around her and the small town at her back. The girl did not see the paddocks, the railway line, the trees, the birds, the clouds. Her eyes were fixed on her own muddy shoes and the boggy road she stalked along.

The crow swooped lower. It laughed its mocking laugh: *waa-waa-waah!* and the girl looked up sharply, scanning the sky with her fists on her hips, as if she dared the bird to jeer again. But then her head dropped.

'Stupid bird,' Sadie muttered to herself. She aimed a pebble at a battered rusting sign beside the narrow track, and then she noticed what it said. *Lake Invergarry.*

Despite herself, her heart lifted. The little town of Boort, where she and her mother had just moved, was built on the shores of Little Lake Boort. That lake was public; it belonged to everybody. People walked their dogs around the circuit track, and Ellie, her mum, jogged around it every morning. In summer, the water teemed with boats and water-skiers, and the caravan park hummed with people, thick as flies, or so Ellie said.

But now Sadie remembered her mum talking about another, private lake, where she and her cousins had gone yabbying every summer. A tucked-away lake, their own secret place. Mum and her cousins had come to Boort every holiday to stay with their grandmother when they were kids, a million years ago. Ellie had loved it; that was why she'd dragged Sadie out of school in the middle of the year to come and live here. She'd just assumed that Sadie would love it too. She'd never even bothered to ask how Sadie felt about it.

Sadie hurled another pebble. It pinged off the signpost to Lake Invergarry, and a little voice whispered in Sadie's head: *you know, it would be pretty cool to have a private lake…*

'All *right!*' said Sadie crossly, and turned down the side track. In the distance she heard the crow again – *wa-aah*, the call drawn out like a sing-song jeer. Crows seemed to be everywhere around here: pecking at road kill, flapping round the lake edge, staring at Sadie with their flat, bright eyes. They gave her the creeps.

She walked doggedly on. She wanted to see the secret lake spread out beneath the cool blue sky, almost like the sea she missed so much. The track rose uphill. Clumps of mud clung to her runners and she began to sweat. At last she reached the low crest of the hill, and gazed down into the shallow valley below.

There was no lake.

The valley was lined with a scum of yellowish mud. The water was gone. It must have vanished years before.

Sadie scuffed along the track until it disappeared. The lake bed had cracked apart into a crust of thick silt the colour of parchment. Sadie poked a cake of yellow mud with her toe and it crumbled into dust. Tussocks of some low clumpy plant with a soft purple feather of a flower had spread across the ground; Sadie had never seen it before.

She wrapped her arms around herself. The only sound was the wind crying in the low trees. She might have been the only person in the world.

The crow called again, a hoarse, creaking lament: *waah…waah…waa-aah…* The sound died away as she walked slowly forward.

At first glance the lake bed had seemed wide and flat and featureless, but now Sadie saw objects thrusting up through the mud: the blackened bones of dead trees and tumbled piles of bricks. There had been buildings there, and bush, before the valley was flooded and everything was drowned. But now the waters had retreated, to reveal what they'd destroyed – a broken-down wall, rotted stumps furred with yellow mud.

A couple of hundred metres from the ruins, Sadie found a cluster of skeletal tree trunks with what looked like crooked sticks scattered beneath them, some upright in the ground as if planted there in echo of the dead trees. As she came closer, she realised they were – or had been – little white crosses.

It was a tiny graveyard. Once a grove of trees would have screened it from view of the buildings, but now the trees were as dead and dry as the bodies buried there, and only a few specks of paint remained on the wooden crosses.

Sadie hastily retreated. How could she have thought that the lake bed was flat and featureless? It undulated, dipped and rose, like the back of an enormous scaly beast, with immense muscles rippling beneath its damp, cracked skin. Lumpy warts of boulders marked the surface.

Waah-waah!

Sadie threaded her way through a knot of blackened tree-skeletons, and found herself in a deeper, hidden hollow. A group of tall stones, a metre or so high, stood in a crooked ring about five metres across.

Her heart was pounding.

The crow called, suddenly almost over her shoulder. *Waaaah*... It was like a command.

Slowly, almost unwillingly, Sadie reached out to touch the nearest of the tall rocks. Her fingertips brushed its rough, crusted surface. The dried mud flaked and crumbled. Sadie rubbed harder with the heel of her hand, and the crust of silt disintegrated and fell away like a scab, exposing smooth, red stone.

Waah! croaked the crow.

Sadie's heart thumped harder. She dug her fingernails under the silt, and, flake by flake, the skin of mud peeled away. She scraped and prised and scratched until the whole tall boulder stood glowing in the cold, clear sunlight. Sadie laid her hand on the rock. It was as warm as a living creature; she could almost feel it breathe.

There were nine boulders in the haphazard circle. Now she'd helped one stone, she had to free the others too. She scraped and scratched and brushed away the dirt until her hands were raw, and sweat poured down her face. She had to clear those silent stones to the air and the sunlight, to let them breathe.

It wasn't until the last rock was clean and Sadie stood back to survey her work, that she noticed the carvings. The marks were almost blurred into the stone: indistinct, powerful, immeasurably ancient. A chill travelled up Sadie's spine like an icy hand, and every hair on her neck stood up.

A crow was there.

It looked like an ordinary bird – black-feathered and with eyes like discs of black glass. It stood on the yellow mud not far from Sadie, its head cocked to the side. It seemed real enough, made of meat and feathers; its feet gripped the mud; its shadow was crisp on the crazed surface of the lake bed. But then it spoke.

It spoke in the guttural *waah wa-ah* of a crow, but Sadie could understand it.

'This is Crow's place.'

Its voice was not angry, but it was stern, and Sadie understood that she must move out of the stone circle. She ducked her head and slipped out between two of the boulders, to stand blinking on the lake bed. She didn't see the crow move, but there it was, in front of her again.

'Crow is awake,' it said. It tilted its head and stared at her with one glittering eye. 'Now it begins.'

Sadie found her voice. 'What begins?'

'Beginning and ending, always the same, always now. The game, the story, the riddle, hiding and seeking, beginning and ending, always.'

'Who are you?' said Sadie. 'Where did you come from?'

The crow opened its beak in a silent laugh, then croaked, '*Waa-waah!* Crow comes from this place; this place comes from Crow. Crow's messengers live here. *Wah!*' It unfurled its wings and shook them out. 'Crow has work for you.'

Sadie's mouth dropped open, but before she could speak, the crow gave one powerful thrust of its wings, rose into the air, and flapped away. In a moment it was out of sight, and the high blue sky was empty.

Sadie's head throbbed and her throat was dry. She looked around, but she couldn't see the crow. She listened for its cry, but the air thrummed with silence.

In a daze, Sadie stumbled back across the lake bed, her shoes heavy with mud. A slender lizard flicked across her path, and she stopped dead, heart racing, in case it spoke to her. *Get a grip!* she told herself fiercely. *You're imagining things to stop yourself dying of boredom. You dreamed it, that's all.*

Or else she was going insane. That was always a possibility. She knew what Ellie would say if she told her she'd had a conversation with a bird. Her mother would be phoning a psychiatrist before Sadie had even finished speaking. That is, if she actually listened to her in the first place. More likely she would just say, *mm, that's nice, darling,* and then launch into some fascinating story of her own...something about how they'd rearranged the fridge at work, or some crazy patient...

The sun slanted into Sadie's eyes, and she realised with a start that it was late in the afternoon. How long had she been at the old lake? She hurried along the deserted track back toward the town – past the pale paddocks that rolled away on either side, blank as empty pages in the weak winter sunlight; across the wide, silent train tracks and the abandoned railway station; past the shabby weatherboard houses scattered beside the road; up the hill along the main street; toward the Railway Hotel and the grey stone soldier on the war memorial.

Sadie had stormed out of the house in the middle of an argument with her mother. When she got back, Ellie would probably yell at her. *Don't you walk out on me when I'm talking to you...* That was the problem; Ellie always talked, she never listened.

Sadie was in no hurry to go home. She lingered beneath the war memorial, reading the inscriptions for the first time. Her own surname leapt out at her.

C. Hazzard, L. Hazzard, W. Hazzard.

Sadie's mum and dad had never married, and Sadie had Ellie's surname. She was glad about that, not just because Dad had left them but because Hazzard was a much more interesting name than Brown. Ellie said there had been Hazzards in Boort forever, and there was the proof, carved into the stone of the memorial.

She circled the pedestal. *A. Mortlock, E. Mortlock, G. Mortlock, T. Mortlock.* More Mortlocks than Hazzards. That was annoying. *A. Murchison, J. Raven, R. Tick, P. Williams.*

There were a lot of names for a tiny place like Boort. Maybe more people had lived here in the olden days when the trains still stopped at the station. Maybe it hadn't always been a dump.

When Ellie announced to Sadie that they were moving to the country, she'd promised trees and creeks and freedom. But instead Sadie had found parched yellow paddocks and empty roads. The mindless screeching of birds, the throb of frogs in the lake. The ominous silence of icy winter nights nudging against the black glass. Endless TV ads for country golf clubs and sheep lice medicine. Personal rubbish tips behind every house, piled with rusting cars and abandoned washing machines and broken prams. The kids at the high school staring at her and ignoring her, thinking she was a snob because she came from the city.

Ellie had found a nursing job at the local hospital. *I can walk to work every day! We'll be able to spend more time together!* But so far Ellie had poured all her energy into trying to make friends with the locals; she didn't have any time left over for Sadie. They might as well have stayed in Melbourne. At least in Melbourne, Sadie had had her own friends to hang out with.

Their so-called new house wasn't that new; at least, it was new compared with most of the decrepit old houses in town. It had belonged to an old lady. It creaked and smelled. Sadie was convinced the old lady had actually died inside it, but Ellie refused to say.

They'd moved in a month before, but to Sadie, it still wasn't home. *Home* was the cream brick house near the sea, where she'd lived all her life. Boort didn't feel like home. Sadie couldn't imagine that it ever would.

They were still camping in the new house, fishing dishes out of boxes and rummaging in suitcases for their socks. Ellie was too busy with her new job to unpack properly, or fix up the house. Sadie's bedroom had hideous flowery old-lady wallpaper.

'Plenty of time to paint later,' Ellie said cheerfully.

Every morning, Sadie woke to that wallpaper, and the light seeping in through an unfamiliar window, and the loss of home punched her in the stomach afresh.

Sadie swallowed the lump in her throat and looked around. The main street was deserted. The distant blare of car horns drifted from the direction of the oval next to the school. There must be a game on; that would be where everyone was.

Sadie paused. She could go and watch the football. There would be kids there from school; someone might say hello.

Ellie would love it if she made some friends in Boort. But Ellie had dragged Sadie to live in the middle of nowhere without consulting her, and Sadie was determined to punish her mother by being as miserable as possible.

Sadie turned her back on the road to the oval.

She'd have to go back to the house; there was nothing else to do.

Perched high in a gum tree, the crow watched as Sadie trailed slowly along the road that ran around the edge of Little Lake. It tilted its head down to look at the roof of the brown brick house, set well back from the water. It saw the girl climb the front steps, lift her hand to the door, and hesitate. It heard a high, cross voice call from inside, 'Sadie? Where have you been?' The girl lifted her chin, pushed open the door, and disappeared inside.

The crow saw the other houses strewn along the shores of the Little Lake and nestled in the shadow of the hill that rose above the town. It saw the jagged grooves of creek beds, gouged into the earth as if scored by a giant stick, and the smooth puddle of the Little Lake, reflecting the blue bowl of the sky. It saw the gnarled fingers of the low, spreading mallee gums beside the lake, the grey and green of ancient scrubland.

New marks had overwritten the oldest signs. The landscape was criss-crossed with roads, railway tracks, electricity towers, boundary fences. When the settlers came, they cleared the land. The remaining trees clustered close to the water, lonely scribbles spelling out their own tale of survival. Houses sprouted like mushroom colonies. New stories were scratched across the land.

But the crow could read the old signs, the old stories. They might be hidden, but they had not vanished. Crow was hidden, too, but he was not gone. Crow was awake. Now it would begin. Crow had a story for the human girl-child. Crow had work for her to do.

Waaah! called the crow. It let itself fall from the branch, as if it might tumble to the ground. Then with one lazy flap of its wings, it rose into the crisp blue air, higher and higher. The green and yellow country rolled below, dotted with trees, snaked across with roads and creeks and fences. The crow circled once, a black mark against the blue. And then it was gone.

As Sadie let herself into the house, Ellie straightened up from the box she was unpacking. Her long fair hair swung over her shoulders, and her green eyes flashed.

'And where did you disappear to? I don't want you running off without telling me where you're going.'

Sadie muttered, 'I thought the whole reason we moved to the country was so I could be a free-range kid.'

'If you want to be free-range, you have to be responsible. Anyway, I need your help. You're thirteen now, you're old enough to pull your weight. You can't expect me to do everything!'

Sadie scowled. 'So I'm old enough to unpack, but I'm not old enough to be consulted on major life decisions like where we're going to live?'

'Don't make me go through this *again*. You know we couldn't possibly afford a house this good in Melbourne – three bedrooms, close to the shops, right beside the lake.'

'Right beside the railway line.'

'Oh, there's hardly been a train go past since we've been here!'

'Just shows how dead this town is,' muttered Sadie.

'It's *lovely* here, Sadie. I've got as much work as I want; I can walk to the hospital; you can walk to school. It's a sweet little town, there's the lake, and the birds. It's beautiful! Just give it a chance, for God's sake.'

'You only came for holidays in the summer. You didn't have to *live* here.'

'Things change, Sadie,' Ellie said sharply. 'You have to learn to adjust. When you were born, I thought I'd never cope, but I did. When your father left, I adjusted. I couldn't sit around sulking and moaning and spreading negativity—'

'I'm *not*,' Sadie growled.

Suddenly Ellie performed one of the lightning about-faces that so charmed other people and made Sadie furious. Ellie dived for her daughter, squeezed her tight and rained kisses on her ear. Sadie struggled to free herself.

'Get *off*, Mum!'

'Let's not fight, Shady-lady! I *hate* it when we fight. I know, why don't we trot down to the oval and watch the end of the football? It's Boort versus Wedderburn. It's the clash of traditional rivals. Possibly.'

'Okay,' mumbled Sadie.

As they trudged past the RSL building on their way to the ground, Sadie said, 'Did you know there are Hazzards on that war memorial outside the pub?'

Ellie laughed and linked her arm with Sadie's. 'Of course. One of them's my grandfather.'

'*Serious?*'

'Clarry Hazzard, your great-grandfather.'

'He was in the war?'

'World War I. He fought in France.'

'Did he get killed?'

'No, he didn't. The memorial is for everyone who went to fight, not just the ones who died. If he'd been killed, I never would have been born and neither would you. No, he came back all right. He married Gran and had four kids and ran the shop across the road from the pub.'

'That little shop on the corner?' Sadie was slightly disappointed. It would have been a much better story if he'd been killed in the war.

'Hey!' protested Ellie. 'It was a great little shop. People used to shop in Boort from miles around, from all the properties in the district. In those days you couldn't just jump in the car and drive to the supermarket, the local shops had to stock everything...' Ellie sniffed ecstatically as they reached the oval. 'Mmm, barbecue! I want a sausage in bread.'

Sausage in hand, Sadie trailed Ellie around the edge of the ground, weaving between spectators until they found a clear space on the fence. A ring of cars was parked inside the fence, on the trotting track that circled the oval.

Ellie poked Sadie in the ribs. 'There's a group of kids. Go and talk to them.'

Sadie squirmed. 'No.'

'You have to make some effort if you want new friends. Chat to people. No one's going to talk to a lump.'

'I am making friends,' Sadie muttered.

Ellie bit into her sausage. 'Yeah?'

'Yeah!'

Sadie turned away to stare at the footballers. A young player in a black-and-white striped jumper leapt into the air, his mop of fair hair flying, and pulled the red ball out of the sky. Cheers erupted and car horns blared around the ground.

A middle-aged couple in black-and-white scarves clapped and whistled wildly. 'Carn the Magpies!' yelled the man. 'Great mark, Lachie!'

The woman glanced at Ellie. 'That's our son. It's his first game in the seniors.'

'*Great* mark,' said Ellie earnestly.

Sadie almost choked on her sausage. Ellie was showing her how to make friends; Sadie knew that her mum knew nothing about football.

Ellie smiled at the woman. 'Is it – it is Amanda, isn't it? You probably don't remember me – Ellie Hazzard.'

The woman looked Ellie up and down. She seemed frosted from head to toe, as if she'd been dusted in powdered ice from her sculpted blonde hairdo to her chilly smile. 'Oh, I remember you.'

'In the *back*!' bawled the man, oblivious to everything but the game. 'Are you *blind*, umpire?'

'And you remember Craig, of course,' said Amanda.

'Oh!' Ellie juggled her sausage, suddenly flustered. 'I didn't recognise – without the hair – hello, Craig.'

The man swung round. He was bull-necked, and shaven-headed to disguise his baldness. He gripped Ellie's hand in his own square, red one. 'Ellie Hazzard. Well, well, well. Heard you were back. Wondered when I'd run into you.'

Ellie laughed uneasily and tried to tug her hand away, but Craig wouldn't let go. She put her other arm round Sadie and pulled her close. 'This is my daughter, Sadie. Sadie, this is an old – an old friend of mine, Craig Mortlock. And Amanda.'

'We got married.' Amanda slid a possessive arm through Craig's and gave Ellie an icy smile.

As if Mum would be interested in her fat old husband! thought Sadie.

'That's our Lachie out in the middle,' said Craig. 'Number 29. Did you see him take that mark?'

Ellie managed to wrench her hand free at last and tucked it safely in her pocket. She and Amanda were both smiling stiff, polite smiles.

'You a football fan?' Craig asked Sadie.

'Not really,' mumbled Sadie.

'We'll have to change that,' said Amanda. 'The football club holds this town together. And the net-ball club, of course.'

'I heard you bought Gwen Reed's place,' said Craig to Ellie.

'I hope you didn't pay too much?' said Amanda.

The three adults began to discuss real estate, and Sadie stopped listening.

She leaned on the fence and stared at the game, not really understanding the action. She found herself watching for number 29, the tall boy with the shaggy fair hair. He was two or three years older than Sadie, younger and skinnier than most of the other players, but he hurled himself at the ball with reckless courage. Even when the older, bigger men trampled him or knocked him aside, he'd scramble up and throw himself at the ball again. Sadie gazed at him, the last bite of her sausage forgotten in her hand.

'*Wah?*' came a voice from behind her. 'You want that?'

Sadie whirled around. A crow stood nearby, watching her with its head on one side. She thought it was a different crow – it seemed smaller, and more ragged, less glossy than the first one – but it was hard to tell.

'*Wah?*' said the crow again, indicating the remains of the sausage.

'Um, sure,' said Sadie blankly, and tossed over the last chunk of charred meat. The crow stabbed it ferociously and gulped it down.

'*Waa-aah!*' said the crow with satisfaction, and flew off with uneven strokes, its wings rustling like taffeta.

'Hey, dreamy.' Ellie was nudging her.

Sadie turned back to find the game had finished and the crowd was streaming away. Little kids spilled over the fence, kicking mini footballs. The air was beginning to chill as the sun slid to the horizon.

'Who won?' said Sadie.

Ellie grimaced. 'The Redbacks whipped us. Hey, guess what? It turns out we are traditional rivals after all. Poor old Maggies.'

In the distance, Sadie saw Boort's number 29 jog up to Craig and Amanda. Craig slapped him on the back and he ducked his head shyly so his hair flopped into his eyes.

'That Lachie's pretty cute,' said Ellie. 'He should be in a boy band.'

'*Mum!*'

Ellie laughed and tucked her arm through Sadie's. 'No law against looking.'

'There were Mortlocks on the war memorial, too,' said Sadie.

'Oh, the Mortlocks own half of Boort. They've got a huge property called Invergarry. I suppose it belongs to Craig now.'

Invergarry. So the dried lake belonged to them...

Sadie said, 'Did you know Craig and what's-her-name when you were kids?'

'Mm. And – later,' said Ellie vaguely. 'Craig asked us back to the pub, actually. But I thought we'd better not.'

'How come?' It wasn't like Ellie to refuse an invitation.

'Oh, you know...busy, busy, unpacking, unpacking...' She released Sadie's arm. 'Come on, I'll race you home.'

Three days a week Ellie was supposed to finish her shift at the hospital in time to walk home with Sadie after school. The school and the hospital were practically next door to each other, but no matter how long Sadie dawdled, Ellie was never ready to leave when she arrived.

On Wednesday Sadie made her way to the emergency department. As usual, there was no sign of her mum. The nurse on duty smiled and said, 'I'll let her know you're here, love.'

'Thanks.' Sadie took a seat and tried not to stare at the only other person waiting – an Aboriginal boy Sadie had seen around at school. He was sitting on the other side of the room, flicking through a magazine. He was in Year 8, a year above her. He was new this term, too; he'd come from Mildura, up on the Murray River. Everyone knew he'd been in trouble with the police, though no one seemed to know exactly what he'd done. Someone said he'd stolen a car, someone else said he'd stabbed a kid in a playground, and someone else that he'd been caught dealing drugs. Everyone agreed he was 'psycho'.

Sadie stared at him from beneath her eyelashes. He had wild curly hair and smudges of shadow under his eyes, and the corners of his mouth turned down. He didn't look like a psycho or a criminal; he looked kind of sad.

'Sadie!' Ellie swooped down on her, smiling and breathless.

'You're late,' said Sadie coldly.

'Sorry, I lost track of time; I ran into someone.' Ellie's eyes were bright, her cheeks flushed. She glanced over her shoulder at a man with pale-brown skin and a wide smile. 'Sadie, this is an old friend of mine, David Webster. He's a social worker; he looks after this whole area. We knew each other years ago. I can't believe I didn't run into him till today! I can't believe he still lives here!'

'Come and gone a bit. Haven't been sitting on my bum by the lake the last twenty years.' David grinned and stuck out a big, warm hand to shake Sadie's.

'How you doing, Sadie?'

'All right,' Sadie mumbled.

'Perk up, sweetheart; I'm not *that* late!' Ellie ruffled Sadie's hair, and Sadie squirmed away, frowning. Ellie rolled her eyes. 'Kids!' She and David smiled at each other.

'I've invited David and his nephew to dinner,' said Ellie. She glanced around and waved to the Aboriginal boy. 'Hey! You must be Walter! Come and say hello; we won't bite. I know, I've got a *great* idea – you can come home with us now while David finishes up here! You had school today, right? You can do your homework at our place, then you and Sadie can hang out together.'

Nooo, thought Sadie in agony.

Walter moved closer to David and almost imperceptibly shook his head. David slung an arm across Walter's shoulders.

'He'll be right with me,' said David easily. 'We'll be along in an hour or so.'

'Oh,' said Ellie. 'Okay. See you soon.'

Sadie stumped behind Ellie back into town, in the direction of the IGA supermarket.

'What's wrong with you?' said Ellie.

'Nothing.'

'Don't crack the sads with me. David's a lovely guy; you'll like him.'

Sadie glared at the pavement.

'And be nice to Walter, okay? You've got a lot in common.'

'Yeah? Has he got a crazy mother too?'

Ellie threw her a sharp look. 'As a matter of fact, his mother isn't very well, so you might want to keep remarks like that to yourself.'

'Okay, *sorry*,' muttered Sadie.

'I meant you're both new in town, that's all. You could help him a lot. Walter's had a hard time. He was in some kind of trouble in Mildura, that's why he's moved here to live with David.'

'Yeah, I know. *Everyone* knows,' said Sadie crushingly. It didn't occur to her till later that she'd missed her chance to find out what, exactly, Walter's trouble had been.

They walked into the IGA and Ellie began searching the aisles for curry ingredients.

'Not as much choice as in Melbourne,' observed Sadie.

Ellie frowned. 'Now listen,' she said, halting suddenly in front of the rice shelf. 'I'm going to tell you something.'

'What?'

'David and I,' Ellie said in a low voice, 'well, we used to go out together.' She glanced about, but there was no one within earshot. 'Years ago, before I met your father. But it was – difficult.'

'Because he's black?'

'Yes, partly. Mostly.' Ellie hesitated, and dropped a packet of basmati rice into the basket. 'It was

– complicated. There was stuff going on. We were young. We just didn't know how to make it work. But we're older now and hopefully wiser.'

'Jeez, Mum, you just met him again five minutes ago. How do you even know he wants to go out with you?'

Ellie laughed. 'He told me he's single. And I picked up a certain vibe. Don't you think there was a certain vibe?' She punched Sadie's shoulder. 'Dontcha reckon? You think I'm rushing things again, don't you?'

Sadie frowned. *Like you rushed into moving to the country. Like you rushed into breaking up with Dad. Like you rushed into asking Walter back to our place when he doesn't even know us.* But she didn't say anything.

Ellie got flustered when she was preparing a big meal; she didn't cook well under pressure. So Sadie wandered down to the end of the backyard. Even though their house was fairly new, it had still accumulated a pile of junk. A dead fridge leaned tipsily against the shed, and an abandoned old ute was slowly sinking into the ground in the shadow of a low-spreading mallee gum.

Sadie climbed into the cabin of the ute, tipped her head back and gazed up at the leaves and the darkening sky through the gap where the roof had rusted away. A pink-and-grey parrot was squawking in the branches of the tree.

'Seen any crows around?' Sadie asked the parrot.

'Nope.'

Sadie jerked upright and banged her forehead.

Walter leaned his arms along the empty window-frame and peered in at her. 'Your mum sent me out here,' he said. 'Said she'd yell when dinner's ready. You all right?'

Sadie gingerly touched her forehead. 'Yeah.'

'C'n I get in?'

'There's only room for one.' Sadie showed him where the driver's seat had been yanked out. She wrenched the door open and clambered out. 'We can sit under the tree if you like.'

Walter shrugged.

Night was beginning to creep across the paddocks beyond the railway track. Sadie hugged her knees and hoped dinner wasn't far away. She picked up a feather from the ground and began to draw on her shoe. With a start she realised it was a crow's feather and dropped it as if it had burnt her.

She knew Ellie would interrogate her later. *Did you talk to Walter? Did you try?* Sadie never knew how to talk to people. Crows: yes. Humans: no.

'So – David's your uncle?' she said awkwardly.

'Yep.'

'You live with him now?'

'Yep.'

'What about your parents?'

Walter shrugged, staring into the dusk. After a minute he said, 'Mum sent me down here. Thought Uncle was the best one to look after me. We got some family round here. Auntie Lily and Auntie Vonn live here in Boort too. You know 'em?'

Sadie shook her head.

'Got some cousins in Wedderburn. Couple more aunties in Kerang.' Walter fell silent. Then he said, 'Things weren't too good in Mildura.'

Sadie didn't know what to say. She wondered if it was true that he'd stabbed someone, but she was too scared to ask. She stared up at the sky. A single star glowed in the depths of blue. She said, 'My dad's out west. He's an engineer with a mining company. He's making heaps of money.'

'Yeah?' said Walter.

'He says he might move to Dubai. Or Africa.'

'Long way.'

'Yeah. But so's the west. And he emails all the time.'

'So you don't need another dad,' said Walter.

'No.'

'And I got my own mum. So I don't need a new mum, either.'

They looked at each other in the gathering dusk; it was getting hard to see. 'Glad we got that sorted,' said Sadie.

Walter made a soft noise that might have been a chuckle. 'Uncle says your real name's Saturday. Reckon he was having a joke with me.'

'No, it's true,' sighed Sadie. 'But no one *ever* calls me Saturday. I *hate* it. It's a *stupid* name.'

'There was a warrior, back when the whitefellas first came. They called him Saturday. He fought for our lands, like a guerrilla fighter. He resisted; he was a hero. Uncle told me.'

Sadie wished she hadn't been so quick to call Saturday a stupid name. 'What happened to him?'

'Got killed.'

'Oh.'

They were silent for a moment. Sadie said, 'Mum had a deal with Dad – if I was a boy, I would have his surname, but if I was a girl, I'd have hers. And I was born on a Saturday, so that's what they called me. It could have been worse. I could have been Anzac or Melbourne Cup.'

'Grand Final?' suggested Walter.

'Or Boxing.'

Walter gave an appreciative snort. He was almost invisible in the dark. He was okay, Sadie supposed, but just because Ellie wanted to go out with David didn't mean she and Walter had to be best friends. The harder Ellie pushed it, the harder Sadie would push back. She could be a resistance fighter, too, like Saturday the warrior...

More stars appeared – silver sparks on blue velvet. The back door creaked open, and David called out, 'Hey, you kids, aren't you freezing your bums off out there? Come in and eat.'

Warmth and brightness and the smell of Ellie's fish curry spilled from the doorway. Sadie didn't exactly elbow Walter out of the way; but she made sure she was the first one inside.

'I can't be bothered cooking tonight,' Ellie announced on Friday night. 'Let's treat ourselves for once and have a meal at the pub.'

Sadie looked up suspiciously from her maths homework, wondering if Ellie was trying to soften her up for something.

Ellie pounced on her, and Sadie shook her off. 'You don't have to *strangle* me.'

Ellie blew a raspberry on Sadie's neck and danced away. Sadie hadn't seen her mum so excited since – well, since she'd decided they were moving to the country. Usually, the only thing that catapulted Ellie into such a good mood was a new project. And this time the new project must be David, Sadie thought sourly. Did he have any idea what he was in for?

Huddled in their parkas, Sadie and Ellie hurried through the frosty night toward the bright lights of the pub. When Ellie pushed open the door, a wave of warmth and noise rolled out to engulf them. It was surprisingly busy for a pub in a speck of a town in the middle of nowhere. Sadie hung back while Ellie pranced in and started chatting away to the old men who propped up the bar, shrugging off her jacket, shaking her long fair hair over her shoulders, laughing and joking with everyone.

Sadie sipped her lemon squash and kept close to her mum's elbow, torn between admiration for her mum's determination to make friends from a roomful of strangers, and a creeping sense of embarrassment. Sometimes, she thought, Ellie tried *too* hard.

Craig Mortlock leaned over and touched Sadie's arm. 'The kids are all out in the back room,' he said.

Sadie clutched her glass, unwilling to leave the protective force field of her mother's presence. But Ellie gave her a nudge. 'Go on. I'll yell when our dinner's ready.'

Sadie scowled, plonked her empty glass on the bar, and stalked away, through the quiet back bar with its pair of shabby leather couches and open fire, past the toilets, and into a low-roofed, draughty extension that opened onto a trellised beer garden.

A jukebox was belting out a daggy old Elton John song, and a group of teenagers clustered round a pool table. Sadie recognised some of them from school, though she wasn't sure of their names. Her heart skipped when she noticed Lachie Mortlock leaning on a cue, talking to an older girl with spiky red hair, the only other girl in the room. The girl saw Sadie, but her eyes flicked away.

Sadie slunk into a dark corner and wished she were invisible. These kids were older than she was; they didn't want anything to do with her at school, and they were ignoring her now. They were all normal kids; birds would never talk to *them*. Sadie wished she was normal. She picked at a pockmark in the wall where the paint had chipped, and watched Lachie and the other boys play pool.

No one spoke to her and after a while she drifted into a kind of peaceful trance. She began to work out names: the goofy boy with the freckles was Nank; the skinny, dark-haired one in the green shirt was Troy. Hammer was the square-headed, loud-voiced boy with no neck; he looked more like Craig's son than Lachie did. The sharp-featured boy with the rat's tail and the earring was Fox.

Sadie forgot that she wasn't really invisible; it was a shock to snap out of her trance and see the red-haired girl in front of her, holding out a cue.

Sadie blinked. 'Sorry?'

'I said, do you know how to play?' The girl smirked over her shoulder at the others. One of the boys guffawed.

'A bit,' Sadie muttered.

The red-haired girl tossed her the cue and racked up the balls. She wore a red tartan miniskirt and black tights with ladders in them. Sadie clutched her cue in a sweaty fist, feeling very small and young. The boys lounged back against the walls, nursing Cokes. Lachie was perched on the back of a vinyl-covered chair. He gave her a smile and a wink, and Sadie's heart flip-flopped. She smiled back.

The red-haired girl messed up her first shot and swore. Nank sniggered. 'Nice one, Jules.'

Sadie lined up her first shot carefully, and potted her ball. She potted the next two before she realised the boys ringed around the walls had fallen silent, watching, and then she got nervous and fluffed the next shot.

'You're not bad,' said Jules grudgingly, and Sadie glowed. She didn't dare glance at Lachie.

Sadie won the game. Lachie and Troy were waiting to play next.

'You're Sadie, right?' said Lachie. His fair hair flopped into his eyes. 'Ellie Hazzard's your mum, yeah?'

Sadie nodded, not trusting herself to speak.

'Thought so. Seen you around school. You should have a look in the front bar some time, and down at the Sports Centre. There are photos of the footy team and the cricket club. Your grandpa Phil's in just about all of them. There's been a Hazzard in every team for the last hundred years, just about. Sporting family, hey? Where'd you learn to play pool?'

'Mum taught me.'

'Yeah, and my dad probably taught *her*.' A knowing laugh ran around the room. Lachie said, 'Give us a game after this one?'

Sadie swallowed; was he serious? She gestured feebly to the front of the pub. 'My mum...dinner...'

'No sweat,' said Lachie. 'Next time, hey?'

'Come on, Lachie, get on with it,' said Troy.

Lachie bent over the table to make his first swift, confident shot. The red ball slammed into the pocket. He winked over his shoulder at Sadie, as if they were two pros together. Sadie's stomach turned inside-out. She didn't even hear Ellie calling her to dinner.

'Was that Lachie Mortlock?' Ellie's eyes danced.

Sadie picked at her peas. 'Mm.'

'It's bizarre seeing Craig and Amanda with a teenage son. I remember when Craig was ten, he had these white-blond curls...' Ellie mimed a halo of hair. 'And now look at him, he's the president of the footy club, head of the progress association… We all used to go down to Lake Invergarry together for yabbies, get plastered in mud. Nana would do her block.'

'I saw the lake the other day,' said Sadie. 'Your lake, I mean. It's all dried up.'

'Really?' Ellie looked up. 'I guess it would be, with the drought. It never was very deep.'

'I saw some ruins sticking up through the mud. They looked like old buildings.'

Ellie popped a sliver of steak into her mouth. 'That would have been the Mortlock's old homestead, where they lived when they first moved into the district. Then someone had the bright idea to flood the valley and turn it into a dam. They built the big new house up on the higher ground. The mansion.' Ellie pulled a face. 'All very grand. I think they had visions of boating parties, picnics, that kind of thing. But the lake was always a dud. It was never much good for anything but yabbies. Just a big, shallow, smelly swamp.'

'When did they build it?'

'I don't know. Ages ago. In the 1920s, maybe?'

Sadie hesitated. 'I thought I saw some – some graves.'

'Did you?' Ellie shrugged. 'There could have been some Mortlocks buried there before they opened the cemetery out on the Wycheproof road.'

'Do you think there are any Hazzards buried at the lake?'

'No way! The Mortlocks wouldn't let any old corpse into their private graveyard. Snobby family, those Mortlocks.'

'They're not snobby now.' Sadie was thinking of Lachie, but she said, 'Craig's very friendly.'

'Yes, well.' Ellie stabbed a potato. 'Amanda, not so much.'

'Do you—' Sadie hesitated again. 'Do you want to go and look one day? At the lake, I mean?'

'No,' said Ellie firmly. 'No thanks.' She propped her cheek on her hand and stared at Sadie. 'It's a spooky place, that lake. To tell you the truth, I never liked it. Even the yabbies tasted weird.'

Sadie didn't answer. Ellie wasn't a superstitious person. She had no patience with ghost stories or fears of the dark or monsters under beds. It was most unlike her to admit to feeling spooked about anything.

'Did you feel it, when you were there?' Ellie said. 'A bad atmosphere?'

'It did feel – strange,' said Sadie.

'Might be a good idea to keep away from there, okay?'

'Mm.' Sadie kept her eyes on her plate.

But she had to know if she'd dreamed the talking crow, if the stones with their mysterious markings were real. Whatever her mother said, she already knew that she had to go back.

'I thought we were going for a walk around Little Lake?' Ellie tapped Sadie's pyjama-clad leg. 'Come on, you're always complaining that we never do anything. Let's go before it rains.'

'It never rains.' Sadie stared at Saturday-morning TV.

'Like my new scarf and hat?' Ellie twirled. 'Black and white, for the Boort Magpies. Gotta show whose side we're on.'

'Crows are better than magpies,' muttered Sadie.

'*Crows*?' squawked Ellie. 'Who are the Crows?' Her phone trilled its cheerful tune and she snatched it from her pocket. Even before she spoke, Sadie could tell from the way she pirouetted from the room that the call was from David. 'Hello!'

Sadie swung her feet from the coffee table and

made a dash for her bedroom. She threw on some clothes and slipped into the hallway. Ellie was sprawled on her bed, phone to her ear. 'So... footy this afternoon?'

Sadie eased the front door shut behind her and set off down the road to the centre of town. The sky was muffled with a layer of grey cloud.

She saw Jules hanging round outside the shops with Fox and the skinny boy who'd played pool with Lachie the night before – Troy. She kept one eye on them as she walked past, pretending not to have seen them in case they ignored her, but Jules raised a languid hand. Sadie gave them a quick wave back, then jammed her hands into her pockets. She marched on, fast and purposeful, down the hill and across the railways tracks.

Lake Invergarry was a mustard-coloured stain, like paint spilled over the landscape. The grey sky lowered over the mud. Dead trees leaned drunkenly from the silt and for an instant Sadie saw them as skeletal hands, groping bony fingers in the air. She halted, feeling lost. She couldn't remember how to find the stones. Had she really dreamed them?

But then a black shadow swooped above her head, gliding under the sky that fitted over the land as snugly as a lid on a box. *Waah – waah!*

Sadie broke into a run, stumbling after the crow, a dark speck against the iron-coloured sky. Clods of mud stuck to her shoes and spattered as she ran.

The crow flung back a long drawn-out *waaaah* that echoed across the valley, and Sadie caught her breath. There was the dip in the valley that hid the secret place from view. And there was the circle of stones, tall and proud, glowing orange-red like columns of flame. And a crow was waiting for her.

Sadie stopped, gasping for breath. The crow watched her, its wings folded back, its eyes gleaming like stars. Silence stretched around them.

After a minute Sadie lowered her eyes. What was she doing here? The crow hadn't spoken, but somehow Sadie knew that it was mutely laughing at her.

At last, the crow opened its beak. Again, its words sounded like *waah-wah*, but Sadie understood. 'This is Crow's place.'

'Yes,' said Sadie. 'You told me that already.'

'Crow has a story for you.'

'Oh,' said Sadie. 'Okay.'

'Sit!' ordered the crow.

'Um…' Sadie looked at the stinking yellow mud. She shrugged off her parka, spread it out and lowered herself gingerly down.

'This is a secret place, a story place.' The crow tilted its head. 'Crow's people came to this place. Now they are gone. The stories are always. Who tells Crow's stories now? Where are the dreams when the dreamers are gone? Where are the stories when no one remembers?'

Sadie didn't know what to say, but it seemed the crow didn't expect an answer.

'Country remembers,' it croaked softly. 'Country remembers. Crow remembers.'

The bird stepped closer, watching Sadie with its bright, cunning eye. She inched back, away from the sharp talons, the strong, gleaming beak.

'This story belongs to Crow. And it belongs to you.'

'To me?' repeated Sadie, startled.

Waah! You come to listen, not to speak!' The crow's eyes closed. Its head dropped.

Sadie waited, her heart beating fast.

At last the crow said, 'Crow cannot see. This is Crow's own place, but he cannot see. The end of this story is hidden in shadow. This is your story, too. You must finish it.' The crow blinked once, twice. 'You do not belong to this place. You do not belong to Crow. But this story is your story.'

Sadie couldn't keep quiet. *What* story?'

'*Waah!*' The crow gave a sudden laugh. 'The story of a clever man!'

'A clever man?' repeated Sadie, bewildered.

'*Wah!* You must be quiet!'

'S-sorry,' stammered Sadie.

'Crow's people know how to listen! Crow's people know how to be still! Your people cannot be silent. Your people cannot sit quiet to listen. There are stories all around you, and you cannot hear! *Waah!* If you cannot listen, Crow must show you!'

Without warning, the crow unfurled its wings. Darkness streamed from beneath its wings, blotting out the earth, blackening the sky. The bird cried, 'You must finish this story. For Crow, and for the spirit of the clever man, which cannot rest!'

Sadie cowered. The crow's wings beat where it stood. Its cries drowned out every other sound, they filled the valley like the roar of thunder, and the ground shook beneath Sadie as she struggled to her feet.

Then the crow's scream rang out, and the bird's talon-feet gripped the earth, slicing into the ground.

Sadie imagined her flesh torn by those talons, her eyes jabbed by that pitiless beak, and she ran.

The sudden night was thick as tar; she didn't know if her eyes were open or shut. Wind whistled and roared about her, screaming with the crow's voice. She didn't know if she was running or falling, dreaming or awake. She was plummeting into the darkness, and the dark was choking her, like soft black feathers in her throat.

S adie was running, her feet striking the ground
with a rhythmic *thud-thud-thud*. She could hear
her own ragged breath, each gasp tearing into
her side like a wound. She was still real, then; she was
still *here*, somewhere, though the darkness was thick as
porridge all around her.

Then she realised she could see a light ahead,
a tiny yellow pinprick no bigger than a solitary star.

She slowed to a jog-trot, shuddering for breath,
and held onto her side where the stitch stabbed her.
Lights glowed above her, too: the silvery dust of
stars, and the thin curve of the moon. The yellow
light ahead was larger now, and square-shaped:
a lighted window. She could make out other shapes
in the shadows, trees and buildings, flares of
lamplight.

She slowed to a walk. *Nothing to be frightened of, you silly duffer*, she scolded herself. *What's got into you? Scared of the Hobyahs?*

She imagined long fingers reaching out of the dark and quickened her pace. She was carrying a basket; she knew that she should carry it carefully. Even when she'd been running full tilt, she'd been careful to balance the basket. She remembered now that it was full of eggs.

She was wearing boots and a frock and her blue cardigan that Gran had knitted, and her hair was tumbling down out of its bobby pins as usual...

And somewhere inside her was Sadie, thinking in amazement, *Who am I? This isn't me! I've turned into someone else!* But somehow she wasn't concerned about this unexpected transformation. She was astonished but not anxious. She walked steadily toward the shop, toward home, the lamplight streaming from the kitchen and the basket of eggs from Mrs Williams on her arm.

She let herself into the stuffy kitchen, warm with the heat of the stove, and set the basket on the dresser. Mum was draining a saucepan of potatoes. John was at the table, bent over his schoolbook, legs wound round the chair legs, tongue poking from the corner of his mouth.

'Bless you, love, you're just in time.' Mum's face

was flushed and a curl of dark hair had escaped from the scarf tied round her head. She wiped her hands on her green-flowered pinafore. 'Mash these spuds, will you? I can hear the baby.'

She whisked out of the room, and Sadie, without thinking, pulled open the right drawer, found a fork and began to mash the potatoes. She looked round for the milk jug and found that and the butter dish on the table. She added milk and butter to the potatoes, beating them to a creamy mash. *Just the way Dad likes them*, she found herself thinking...

Sadie knew that these weren't her thoughts, they belonged to someone else. She wondered, without panic, whose thoughts they were, whose life she had stepped into.

The plates were warming in the bottom of the oven, the mutton and gravy were ready, the beans boiling on the stovetop. *Don't overcook the beans!* thought Sadie, and an echo of Ellie's voice flashed through her mind. *Vegies boiled to death, yuk...* She snatched up the saucepan and drained the water, tipped the beans into a dish and looked around for a bottle of olive oil to drizzle over them.

Olive oil? Sadie frowned. Whatever put an idea like that into her head? She'd never heard of such a thing. She dropped a knob of butter on the beans and stared at them doubtfully. Mum was going to say they were half-raw.

Sure enough, when Mum bustled into the kitchen with the baby grizzling on her shoulder, she picked up a bean and bit into it. 'Still crunchy, love! You took them out too soon.'

'I like them crunchy,' said Sadie. 'And if you cook them too long they lose all their vitamins...'

'Hark at her!' said Mum. 'Vitamins indeed. Clear off the table, Johnny, and set the plates.' She leaned out of the doorway and called, 'Clarry! Dinner! Now then, where's your sister? Betty, if you're hiding again, you come out now, you hear me?'

Clarry. That name seemed familiar...How did she know that name? She shook her head. Of course she knew the name of her own father! What in the world was the matter with her tonight?

As Sadie whipped the newspaper off the table, an upside-down headline caught her eye – something about a person called Hitler. Her heart gave a peculiar involuntary skip. The date was printed at the top of the page. *Friday, June 23, 1933.*

Mum took the paper from her hands. 'What's wrong, love? You look poorly all of a sudden.'

'I feel a bit faint,' whispered Sadie, groping for the back of a chair.

'You sit down, I'll dish up. Ran back from

Williams's too fast, I daresay. There, can you hold the baby? Betty, have you washed your hands?'

A little girl of about five or six peered from behind a curtain of dark hair at Sadie, who sat with the heavy, drooling baby on her knee, one hand pressed to her forehead. John moved silently around the table, doling out the plates.

'I can help, I can!' Betty clattered the knives and forks beside the plates; Sadie winced at the noise.

'Forks on the left, don't you know that yet?' grumbled John.

Mum paused to lay her hand on Sadie's brow.

'You want to go and lie down, pet?'

'No – no, I'm fine.' Sadie managed a smile. 'I think I just need my dinner.' She realised she was ravenous; she remembered that she hadn't had any breakfast before she rushed out this morning, before she saw the crow...

The world seemed to slide sideways for an instant as Sadie struggled to match up two sets of memories, two versions of herself. But then Clarry came into the room and everything steadied. Dad seemed to radiate a kind of calm. As he entered the kitchen, the children stopped bickering and sat up straight; Mum looked up and smiled; even baby Philip's grizzling faded and he held up his arms for a cuddle.

Sadie took her place at the table and picked up her knife and fork.

'What about grace, Sadie?' said Dad mildly, and Sadie blushed as she bowed her head for the prayer. How could she have forgotten about grace?

Afraid of making another mistake, she was quiet for the remainder of the meal. Betty told a long story about an episode of unfairness at school, and baby Philip spattered mashed potato from his wooden high chair. Everyone teased Sadie about the under-cooked beans. John said, 'You trying to turn us all into rabbits?'

But Dad said solemnly, 'I don't know that I don't prefer them with a little crunch, after all,' and he winked at Sadie.

'She's not herself,' said Mum. 'She needs a dose of cod liver oil, I shouldn't wonder.'

Betty grimaced and gagged.

'That's enough from you, miss, or you'll have some too,' said Dad, and Betty subsided with a wriggle and a pout.

After dinner and a spoonful of the revolting fishy oil, Mum made Sadie sit in the chair by the stove while she put the little ones to bed. Dad and John washed up, talking about cricket. Sadie let her eyelids droop. She seemed to drift far, far away, to another world entirely, a world of incessant noise and bright lights…

And then she was dreaming. She was swept into a place where the night was thick as treacle, a place of fire and song and strange swirling dances. And a black-feathered figure loomed out of the dark, and its sharp beak opened, and its scream rang out.

S adie jolted awake. Her head whirled. She was still sitting by the stove, but her body ached as if she'd travelled a hundred miles and back.

John must have gone to bed. Mum and Dad were at the table, Dad reading one of his library books while Mum checked through the accounts, pencil in hand. With her dark hair freed from its scarf and her pinny hanging behind the door, she looked young. Of course, she was young, compared to Dad. Dad was old, grey-haired and stiff in the leg where he'd been wounded. He must have seemed like an old man to Mum even when he first came back from the War. She was nineteen then. *Not that much older than me*, thought Sadie. *Why on earth did she decide to marry him?*

But even as she watched, Mum's hand crept across the tabletop, and Dad's hand captured it. He kissed her fingertips, and they smiled at each other, tender in the lamplight. Sadie looked away, knowing it was a private moment, but glad, in a peculiar, embarrassed way, that she had seen it.

There was a tap at the back door.

Dad pushed back his chair and limped to open it.

For an instant, Sadie thought that the night itself had come into the kitchen, breathing its chill breath over them all; she blinked and saw the black-feathered bird-figure from her nightmare. And then she relaxed back into her chair and laughed at herself, because it was only Jimmy Raven, the Mortlocks' stockman, who she'd known all her life. Jimmy was her friend, certainly no one to be frightened of.

He shook Dad's hand, nodded to Mum and flicked a half-smile to Sadie where she sat curled in her chair, hidden in the shadows. He saw her, though Mum and Dad seemed to have forgotten she was there. She wasn't entirely sure herself that she *was* there; perhaps she was still dreaming.

Dad pulled out a chair. 'Care for a beer, Jimmy?'

Mum laughed. 'You ought to know by now, Jimmy never touches the stuff. How about a cup of tea?'

'Just being hospitable, Jean,' protested Dad, with a wink, and Sadie thought that Jimmy might laugh his deep rolling laugh that echoed halfway across the town. But he just grinned a little and sat down – too big for the frail chair, too big for the small kitchen – and laid his hat on the table.

In her dreamy, detached state, Sadie was aware of everyone's thoughts, even though they didn't speak a word. She saw Mum and Dad exchange a glance and knew they were wondering what Jimmy had come for; he'd never come calling after dark before. And she knew, watching Jimmy as he clasped and unclasped his big, calloused hands, his eyes cast down, that he wanted to talk over something important but didn't know how to begin.

Mum asked after Netta and the children, and received polite replies, and Dad fetched out the good teacups, the thinnest china with the ivy pattern round the rim. Sadie knew that there was no one else in town, in the whole district, who would bring out the best china to serve a black stockman a cup of tea, and a strange feeling struggled in her, between pride and shame.

The three adults sipped their tea and talked about the weather, and at last, long last, Jimmy set down his fragile teacup carefully on its saucer, and said, 'I want to talk to you, Lofty.'

A shiver ran down Sadie's spine. Lofty had been Dad's nickname in the Army, because he was short. That was how soldiers' nicknames worked, Dad said. Blue for a bloke with red hair; Slim for a fat man. Jimmy and Dad had fought together in France; Dad said Jimmy had saved his life. They were mates in the War. That was why Dad brought out the best china.

And that was why Dad had fought the whole town council, when the war memorial was built, to have Jimmy's name put on it, too. They said it couldn't be done, because Jimmy hadn't enlisted in Boort; he'd joined up down in Melbourne. But Dad said he belonged in Boort as much as anyone, and deserved to have his name up there with the rest. After all, Bert Murchison had joined up in Melbourne, too, and no one said *he* should be left off.

At last, Mr Mortlock had backed up Dad, and that was the end of that. No one in Boort dared to argue with Mr Mortlock. He'd fought in the War with Dad and Jimmy, too. And, after all, he was the one who'd given Jimmy a job at Invergarry when the War was over.

Even so, Sadie was sure that Mr Mortlock had never given Jimmy tea in the best china. Only Dad did that.

But Jimmy was always very polite, and called Dad 'Mr Hazzard', even if there was no one else around. This was the first time, the only time, Sadie had ever heard him call Dad 'Lofty'.

Dad pushed away his cup. 'Spit it out then.'

Jimmy hung his head, and his sigh seemed to come up from the bottom of his boots. 'It's like this, see.' He was silent for a long moment. Then he said, 'Suppose you're given something to look after. Something precious, something—' He glanced across at Dad. 'Something sacred. And suppose you knew that a person was planning to do something that would destroy that sacred thing. What would you do?'

Dad considered. 'I'd have to move that thing to somewhere safe, wouldn't I?'

Jimmy's grin split his face for a second, then he shook his head. 'Can't move this thing.'

'Well, what about—' Dad began, but he was interrupted by another knock at the back door. This time it was not a polite tap, but a peremptory rapping.

'Excuse me,' said Dad. 'It's like Flinders Street Station in here tonight.'

He opened the door and a tall, long-limbed man pushed his way into the kitchen, removing his hat to reveal wispy fair hair, high on his forehead. He stopped abruptly when he saw Jimmy seated at the table, and curved his lips in a cold smile.

'Evening, Jean, Clarry. Didn't realise you already had company.'

'You're welcome to join us,' said Dad. 'Jeannie's just brewed up, there's plenty left in the pot.'

'Wouldn't want to impose.' The man's mouth twisted, just short of a sneer, and Sadie knew who it was now, of course; it was Mr Mortlock, Gerald Mortlock, the boss of Invergarry. The boss of Boort, some said. Jimmy Raven's boss.

Jimmy rose to his feet, knocking aside the chair that seemed so spindly beneath his powerful body. He jammed on his hat and stepped to the door.

Clarry put out his hand. 'Don't go, Jimmy.'

And Jean said, 'Jimmy, there's no need to go. Stay and finish your tea.'

But Jimmy, head down, mumbled something about it being late, and an early start tomorrow, and before anyone could stop him, he'd slipped out into the night. The room seemed much emptier without him.

Dad was still standing, holding onto the back of his chair. But Mr Mortlock dragged a chair toward himself and swung it around one-handed. He sat down with his boots stretched out in front of him and began to roll a cigarette.

'Hope Jimmy's not making a nuisance of himself,' he said.

Dad said, 'Jimmy's always welcome here.'

Mum said softly, 'We don't smoke in this house, Gerald. Clarry's lungs, you know.'

'Oh! Pardon me, I was forgetting.' Mr Mortlock

made a great show of tucking away his silk tobacco pouch inside his jacket. 'What was he doing here, anyway?'

'Jimmy sometimes drops in for a yarn,' said Dad.

'Jolly good, jolly good.' Mr Mortlock smoothed the back of his head. 'But you do know, Clarry, the War's over. It's been over for a good few years. We're not in the trenches now.'

'Thank God,' said Dad.

Mr Mortlock wagged his finger at him. 'Now, I backed you over the Memorial, Clarry, because it was the right thing to do. He fought with the best of us, and I've never denied that. You know I've done what I could for him. He's a good man, a good worker, always said that. But *I've* always known where to draw the line, Clarry. Unlike some.'

He stared across the table at Dad, and Dad gazed back. There was a silence.

At last Mum said, 'Was there anything particular you wanted, Gerald?'

Mr Mortlock smiled. 'As a matter of fact,' he drawled. 'I need a box of matches.'

Mum pressed her lips together. Then she hurried from the kitchen through into the closed, darkened shop at the front of the building. A moment later she was back, a matchbox on her outstretched palm.

'Thank you very much,' said Mr Mortlock, and he rose and set his hat on his head. He touched the brim to Mum. 'Lovely as ever, Jean. You're a lucky man, Clarry Hazzard.'

'I know it,' said Dad. His knuckles were white where he gripped the back of his chair.

'Hooroo,' said Mr Mortlock, and the door banged shut behind him.

Dad let out a long breath and sank into his chair.

Mum stood behind him and placed her hands on his shoulders. 'He didn't pay for the matches. I'll put it on the Invergarry account.'

'No,' said Dad. 'Leave it.'

'But—'

'No!' said Dad. 'Leave it be.' He laid his hand on Mum's. 'We were all mates together, over there,' he said, in a slow, heavy voice. 'The three of us. When did it change, Jean? Why did it have to change?'

'That's the way the world is,' said Mum.

'We made a promise in France, the three of us. We promised if we made it out of there alive, we'd look after each other.'

'I know,' Mum whispered. She kissed his grey hair, and rested her chin on the top of his head. For a long while they stayed there without moving.

Then Mum seemed to shake herself awake. 'Sadie? Are you still there?' She looked directly across at Sadie. 'Are you feeling better, pet?'

Sadie stirred in the big chair, the first time she'd moved for hours, or so it seemed. She opened her mouth to say that she felt fine, that she was going to bed.

But before the words could leave her lips, the world darkened around her, and she felt a rush of wind. A sudden blinding light exploded around her. Sadie cried out and squeezed her eyes tight shut against the glare.

Sadie pressed her hands to her eyes, then cautiously let herself blink through her fingers.

It was broad day. She was sitting on the mud of the lake bed, her jeans and parka smeared with muck. The grey sky was drawn over the dried lake like a blanket tucked over a bed.

Sadie moaned. Her head was spinning.

A dead tree poked from the silt. A long scoop of bark was missing from its trunk, leaving a deep scar shaped like a vertical eye. A crow – the same crow? – perched on one empty branch, its head tilted down to Sadie.

She was staring at the scarred tree when the crow dived, a silent missile, straight for her head. Sadie ducked, flinging up her arms, and with a rush of feathers the crow spread its wings and swooped up and away, flapping steadily into the sky. Only the

croaking echo of its laughter floated back to where
Sadie sprawled on the yellow mud.

Your story!

Wah-wah-waaaaah!

S adie stumbled home, grubby and chilled.

Ellie's mouth dropped open. 'Where the *hell* have you been? I was worried sick! We're going to the footy, it starts at two-thirty. Are you all right?'

Sadie stood dumbly, not knowing whether to nod or shake her head. Ellie grabbed her, half-hugged, half-shook her, and thrust her into the bathroom. 'You're filthy. Quick, have a shower. Only you could get covered in mud in the middle of a fifteen-year drought! What have you been doing, rolling in it?'

Under the spray of warm water, Sadie looked down at herself and shivered. For a few hours, she'd left this body; she'd inhabited someone else's body, someone else's life.

Already the events of the night were fading, dream-like, from her mind, but she clutched at the few facts she was certain of. Her father had been Clarry, her mother was Joan – no, Jean. Her own name had still been Sadie – hadn't it? She was sure they'd called her Sadie... She'd had a little sister and two brothers: Betty and John and baby Philip.

Ellie's grandfather was called Clarry. And her father's name was Phil.

Sadie could dimly remember Grandpa Hazzard – a gaunt, kindly figure with teeth too big for his mouth. Nothing like the pudgy, solid infant who'd sat, dribbling and vaguely damp, on her lap.

So the crow had sent her back into the past, to live one night in the history of her own family. But why?

Your story.

Sadie turned off the tap and pressed the towel to her face. Her head was still spinning.

The football match was in Wycheproof, forty minutes drive away. As soon as she stepped out of the car, Ellie spotted a group from the Boort footy club and headed over, smiling and waving. Sadie trailed behind her. She didn't feel like talking to anyone. She was relieved to see the Mortlocks on the far side of the oval, and Jules and the rest of the pool-playing gang over near the change rooms, a safe distance away.

Sadie leaned against the fence and stared blankly as the game began, letting her mind drift, stray thoughts connecting and separating. There had been a Mortlock in her dream – or vision, or whatever it was. Gerald Mortlock. Sadie saw a sudden vivid image of his long, pale fingers toying with a black silk tobacco pouch.

'Hey.'

She turned, startled, as Lachie Mortlock draped himself over the rail beside her.

'Hi.' Sadie revised her decision not to talk to anyone; *anyone* didn't include Lachie. She wished she'd worn her blue top, the one Mum said brought out the colour of her eyes. She poked her hair nervously behind her ear. 'Jules and Nank and Fox are over there,' she volunteered, out of some insane desire to be helpful. She could have kicked herself. She didn't want him to go over there.

'Yeah, thanks, I know.' Lachie directed a brooding glare at the middle of the ground where the tallest players were scrabbling for the ball. 'Jules is all like, *oh, poor Lachie!*' He put on a whiny voice. *'Aren't you disappointed you had to play in the reserves this week?'* He kicked at the fence. 'She doesn't get it, you know? I was lucky to get picked last week. Muz is back now, that's the way it goes. You can't whinge about it like a kid. And it's not my fault we lost today. Boort reserves team is crap. Just like the seniors.' He kicked the fence.

Sadie kept quiet.

Lachie heaved a sigh. '*Anyway*... You going to give me that game of pool some time?'

'Um, yeah. Sure.'

'How about right now? Better than watching the Magpies get belted again.'

'*Now?*' squeaked Sadie. 'But we're in Wycheproof!'

'They have pool tables in Wycheproof, you know.' The corners of Lachie's eyes crinkled when he smiled. He had the bluest eyes. 'But yeah, you're right, they might not let us into the pub. Not you, anyway. How old are you?'

'Fourteen,' said Sadie. 'Practically.' She was mortified.

'Yeah? Seriously?' Lachie kicked the fence again; the whole length of wire vibrated. 'BALL!' he yelled without warning. 'Oh, crap. BALL! I can't watch this,' he said abruptly. He turned his back and dug his hands into his pockets. 'I'm going home.'

Sadie stared. 'Your dad won't leave, will he? Isn't he the president of the club or something?'

'I don't need Dad. I've got my bike. Come and look.' He strode away without a backward glance. Sadie followed, prepared to admire any old bicycle if it belonged to Lachie.

'There,' said Lachie proudly. It wasn't a bicycle; it was a trail bike. 'It's new. Birthday present.'

'Wow,' said Sadie. 'Don't you have to be eighteen to ride one of those?'

Lachie grinned. 'Not on private property. I can ride it round the farm as much as I want.'

'But − we're not on the farm now.'

'Nah. But who's going to arrest me? The police round here all know me.' He patted the seat. 'Want a ride?'

Sadie swallowed. 'I don't think my mum…'

The scowl reappeared on Lachie's face. 'Well, if *Mummy* won't let you…'

'Where would we go?' said Sadie hastily.

Lachie shrugged. 'I dunno. Know anywhere worth going?'

'What about your lake?'

'My lake? Yeah, jeez, it's great, isn't it. Real tourist attraction.'

'What about the stones?'

The words were out of her mouth before she could call them back. Far off in the distance, she heard a crow's mournful cry. *Waaa-waaah*…

Lachie frowned. 'What stones?'

'There's a circle of stones − big ones, with carvings…' Sadie's voice faltered.

'Yeah? Where?' Lachie was interested now. 'Can you show me?'

'I – I guess.'

'I'll bring you back before your mum even knows you're gone,' said Lachie. 'You can wear my helmet.' He held it out enticingly, a round black fishbowl. Sadie lowered it onto her head and staggered under its weight. She thought her neck might snap; she could barely see. Lachie laughed. 'I hate wearing that thing! I don't need it anyway. Up you get.'

A moment's scramble, and Sadie found herself on Lachie Mortlock's motorbike, her arms round his waist, her thighs wedged against his. She could feel him breathe; she could feel his muscles ripple as he moved. *Please God, don't let me fall off*, she prayed, not because she was afraid of getting hurt, but because it would be so humiliating.

Lachie revved the engine and then they were speeding down a dirt track, bumping over ruts. Trees flashed past; paddocks streamed by in a blur.

Sadie's arms ached, her bum felt bruised. Ellie would surely notice she was missing; she'd be in trouble again. The noisy drone of the engine vibrated through her head.

At last they reached the lake. Clots of yellow mud spurted under the bike's wheels. Lachie yelled something, but she couldn't hear. She guessed he was asking directions, and she flung out her arm. He swerved the bike, and Sadie leaned, terrified,

almost parallel with the ground. Lachie straightened the bike, and though she couldn't hear it, she
knew he was laughing by the way his ribs vibrated
under her hands.

She managed to indicate the cluster of dead trees
that surrounded the hollow. Lachie drew up the
bike and killed the engine. Sadie clambered down,
her knees knocking. She lifted off the helmet and
suddenly she could see and hear and breathe again.

'There,' she said shakily.

Lachie walked up to the ring of stones. He peered
at one, then another. He walked slowly right around
the circle.

'Holy crap,' he said softly. 'I never knew this was
here. I never saw them before. Looks like an old
burial site or something.'

'Not a burial site,' said Sadie, surprised by her
own certainty. 'It's not for that.'

'Yeah? What's it for, then?'

A secret place. A story place, the crow had said. 'I – I
don't know,' said Sadie.

Her legs shook; her whole body was racked with
shudders. She wrapped her arms round herself.
Maybe she had motion sickness from the swooping
journey on the bike. She was terrified she might throw
up. She never should have brought Lachie here; she
should have protected the secret. *Crow's place.*

'Lachie,' she said, with sudden desperation. 'Listen, you can't tell anyone about this place.'

'Secret women's business, is it? Secret men's business? Secret kids' business?' He was laughing at her. Then his face softened. 'Okay, mate. It's your special place, is it? I won't tell anyone.'

Not my special place, thought Sadie. *It belongs to the crows.* But she didn't say it aloud.

Lachie tipped up her chin and gazed into her eyes. Sadie thought she might faint. 'So now it's our special place, okay? Our secret?'

Sadie nodded. She could hear crows cawing angrily somewhere in the distance, but she didn't care. Her heart was singing; she had a secret to share with Lachie Mortlock.

T hey were back just in time to see the Wycheproof Narraport Demons defeat the Boort
Magpies by five goals. The Wycheproof crowd
whooped and whistled and flourished their blue-
and-red scarves; the Boort supporters wound their
black-and-white scarves round their necks and hunched
into them. They dispersed swiftly, jangling their keys
and muttering, 'See you back at the pub.' The slam
of car doors reverberated round the oval, and a line of
vehicles soon streamed down the Boort road.

Ellie squeezed Sadie's shoulders. 'What happened
to you? I couldn't find you at half time.'

'Hanging out with some kids,' mumbled Sadie.

'Oh *good*! I knew you'd make friends if you kept
trying. Well, I don't mind sharing you if I have to.'
Ellie checked her watch. 'I told David to be at our

place at six. I thought we could take him to dinner at the pub.'

Sadie turned away to hide a sudden smile. Lachie would be at the pub. Maybe tonight they'd play that game of pool. Maybe he'd call out, *Hey, Sadie!* for everyone to hear. Maybe he'd throw his arm around her shoulder and draw her inside the charmed circle in the pool annexe, and she'd become one of the gang. After this afternoon, anything seemed possible...

But Sadie's heart dropped when Walter sidled through their front door behind David. Now she'd be expected to look after him instead of hanging out with Lachie. She could tell Ellie hadn't expected Walter either, from the extra-warm smile she put on when she saw him, and the way she ushered him into the living room with her hand on his back. 'Isn't this lovely!' she said brightly.

Walter stared at the carpet.

'I thought we'd go down to the pub! We had a great meal, didn't we, Sadie? Local sausages and steak, and the chips were to die for. It's the place to be in Boort on a Saturday night. Not that there's a *massive* amount of competition...'

David hesitated. 'If you want to.' He glanced at Walter and Sadie. 'Would you guys rather stay here?'

Ellie punched his arm. 'Of course they'll come! Are you trying to get me on my own? Is that your cunning plan?'

Walter muttered, 'I don't care.'

'I want to come,' said Sadie, glaring.

David's shoulders twitched inside his leather jacket in the slightest of shrugs. 'Okay.'

Sadie and Walter walked in silence behind David and Ellie along the darkened road. The steady chirp of the frogs floated to them from the lake's edge. David had his arm round Ellie's waist, and fragments of conversation floated back to the others.

'...thought it would take ages to fit in,' Ellie was saying. 'But everyone's been so friendly.'

'Because you had family here...' David murmured. '...not really strangers...'

'I feel as if we really *belong* here, you know? Like we've come home.'

Speak for yourself, thought Sadie, but then she remembered Lachie, and a glow of warmth melted her bitterness away. Maybe, just maybe, one day Boort might feel like home to her, too.

Just past the war memorial lay the low silhouette of what used to be the Hazzards' shop. A sudden wave of giddiness washed over Sadie and she stumbled.

'You okay?' said Walter.

'Yeah. Just tripped on a stone.'

The pub was bright and noisy, filled with drinkers and music and the smell of beer. A fire roared in the back bar, and the jukebox blared from the annexe where the pool table stood. Sadie could just hear the click of balls through the hubbub, and a distant *whoar!* as someone potted a tricky shot.

Heads turned as they entered. That always happened when someone came into the pub. Then people would either smile and nod *g'day*, or if they didn't know you, they'd turn back and resume their conversation.

But Sadie realised immediately that something was different. People looked round. They stopped talking. They stared, and their neighbours turned to stare too. Sadie felt as if the whole pub had fallen silent, watching them.

'I'll get the drinks.' Ellie bounced up to the bar as if she hadn't noticed anything wrong.

David shrugged off his leather jacket and hooked it on his finger. 'Warm in here, eh?'

Walter ducked his head and stuck to David's side like a burr. Sadie's heart was thumping. The noise level hadn't dropped much; she knew that everyone in the pub couldn't have gone quiet, but she felt as if a spotlight had been trained onto their little group of two white females and two black males. Craig Mortlock muttered something, and someone sniggered, and though Sadie couldn't hear what he'd said, her face burned.

'Two beers and two lemonades,' announced Ellie, her hands full of glasses. 'It's a bit quieter in the back bar, why don't we look at the menu in there?'

Her chin was up. Her cheeks were pink and her eyes were bright. Sadie knew that her mother had noticed the stares and the muttering.

Once they'd left the front bar, the hum of conversation and laughter rose again. They perched on the two worn leather couches in front of the fireplace, and Sadie gazed unseeing at a menu. The print swam before her eyes. David murmured to Ellie, and Ellie said loudly, 'I'm okay if you are.'

'I'm okay,' said David. He sipped his beer, surveying the room over the rim of his glass. His eyes caught Sadie's, and he gave her a swift wink. Sadie found herself smiling back. Her heart stopped thudding; when she looked down at the menu again, the print sprang into focus.

'I'm having the sausages,' she said. 'The sausages are really excellent.'

'Didn't you have a sausage at the footy?' protested Ellie.

'No,' said Sadie. 'Anyway, it wouldn't count. They're practically different food groups. *These* sausages have actual meat in them.'

David laughed. 'Sausages sound good.' He spread his arms across the back of the couch and stuck his boots up on the low table. He didn't care if people muttered and stared; he knew he had as much right to be there as anyone. He looked strong, invincible, like a warrior.

Suddenly Sadie wanted to show him that she could be as brave and bold as he was. She jumped up. 'Want a game of pool?' she asked Walter.

Walter glanced at David. David gave a slight nod. Walter stood up and followed Sadie, his hands jammed in his pockets, his head down.

The annexe was almost empty. No one was playing. The whole gang was outside in the beer garden, gathered round Troy, looking at something. A gust of laughter exploded from them, and for a second Sadie wished she were out there with them all, standing beside Lachie, included in the joke. She heard Jules's scornful cry, 'Get lost, Fox!' and everyone sang *ooooh!*

'Do you want to play or what?' said Walter.

Sadie turned her back on the gang and racked up the balls. Walter watched her, hands in his pockets.

'Grab a cue,' said Sadie, and when he didn't move, she tossed him one. 'We don't have to play if you don't want to.'

Walter shrugged. 'I don't care.'

'Do you know how?'

He shrugged again. 'Sort of.'

Sadie explained the rules and took first shot, but she missed and the ball ricocheted uselessly off the cushion. Walter hefted his cue awkwardly onto the table, lined up and thrust. The ball shot straight into the pocket.

Sadie gaped. 'I thought you couldn't play!'

'Thought wrong, didn't ya,' said Walter with a grin, and lined up his next shot.

Sadie didn't even notice that the gang had trooped back inside until Jules tapped her on the shoulder and jerked her thumb. 'You kids – off.'

'We're nearly finished,' said Sadie.

'You are finished. Now.'

Sadie glimpsed Lachie at the back of the room, one foot propped against the wall, his head lowered. 'We'll only be a minute,' she said.

Lachie glanced up, and for one glorious moment Sadie thought he was going to stride over and pull Jules away. *Leave her alone, guys. Because I say so.* Lachie smiling down, their eyes meeting, just like this afternoon, only this time everyone would see . . .

Lachie pushed himself off the wall and strolled to the pool table. 'Come on, kids,' he drawled. 'You heard Jules. Your turn is *over*.' He didn't even look at Sadie; he was staring at Walter.

Walter didn't move. His eyes were down, his hands wrapped round the cue. Maybe he thought if he ignored them they would go away.

Lachie leaned forward. He tried to prise the cue from Walter's fingers. 'Did you hear me? I *said*, get lost.'

Walter didn't let go. He raised his head and stared into Lachie's eyes. 'You should watch out, mate,' he said in a low voice. 'Bad things happen to people who piss me off.'

'Is that right?' said Lachie.

Walter smiled. 'Didn't you hear about what I did in Mildura? Put a policeman in hospital.'

'Yeah, sure you did.'

Walter leaned forward. 'With the power of my *mind*.'

'Bull,' said Lachie, uncertainly.

Walter shrugged. 'You believe what you want. I put a curse on this guy. They reckon he might learn to walk again by Christmas. If he's lucky.'

'You're full of it,' said Lachie. But he let go of the cue.

Walter tossed it onto the table. 'We were finished anyway.'

'No, we weren't!' said Sadie. 'This isn't fair!'

'Life's not fair.' Jules wrenched Sadie's cue from her. 'Go on, piss off with your abo boyfriend.'

A ripple of nervous laughter ran around the annexe. Sadie heard someone mutter *something-lover*.

'Like her mother,' murmured someone else.

'*What?*' Sadie swung round, clenching her hands into fists. '*What* did you say?'

'C'mon, Sadie,' said Walter. 'They're not worth it.'

Lachie slung a cue across his shoulders, hooked his arms over it and swaggered around the table. Troy whispered to Fox and they sniggered together.

Walter suddenly lunged for them, wiggling his fingers and making spooky noises, and they both jumped back, swearing.

Walter snorted. 'See you round, tough guys.'

Sadie followed him out of the annexe. She was almost crying with rage. 'Don't you just want to *hit* them?'

Walter shrugged. 'Nah. There're better ways.'

'You didn't – you didn't really curse that man, did you?'

Walter didn't answer, but he threw her a look over his shoulder and raised one eyebrow.

David and Ellie were still sitting by the fire. They weren't speaking. David was drumming his fingers on the arm of the couch, and Ellie's lips were pressed together.

Ellie attempted a smile. 'Who won?'

'We did,' said Walter.

David stood up. 'They're calling our number. Let's eat.'

They left as soon as the meal was finished. 'No point paying for coffee when I can make one just as good at home,' said Ellie; but Sadie knew the real reason was that they all wanted to escape as quickly as possible.

Sadie would have liked to go to bed; it had felt like the longest day of her life. But she couldn't because Walter was there. They sat staring at the football on TV while Ellie and David disappeared into the kitchen to make the coffee.

After a few minutes Walter said, without taking his eyes from the screen, 'They're arguing.'

'What?' Sadie shot an alarmed glance toward the sliding door that separated the living room from the kitchen. 'I can't hear anything.'

Walter stared at the TV. Sadie slipped out of her chair and tiptoed to the door.

She heard Ellie's voice, a little shriller than normal. 'That's ridiculous! That was *years* ago.'

Then David's voice, slightly louder. 'So what do *you* think was going on tonight?'

'Isn't it obvious? You – and me – some people have trouble with it, you must know that by now.'

'Sure, but there's more to it than that in this town. I didn't want to go to the bloody pub in the first place.'

'Well, why didn't you *say* so?' Ellie's voice rose.

David responded with a furious muttering that Sadie couldn't make out. She crept back to her seat.

A moment later, David emerged from the kitchen, his face stern. He said to Walter, 'Come on, mate. We'd better go; it's getting late.'

Sadie scrambled up. Ellie stood in the kitchen doorway, her eyes red, her chin thrust up.

'See ya,' said Walter.

'Yeah,' said Sadie.

When David and Walter had gone, Ellie collapsed into a chair and sank her head in her hands. 'Grr!' She tore at her hair. 'I handled that *so well*,' she said in a muffled voice. She looked up ruefully at Sadie. 'Sorry, sweetheart. Did you hear us?'

'A bit.'

Ellie sighed. 'I should probably tell you—'

Sadie gazed at the TV. She wasn't sure if she could handle any more drama today.

Ellie said, 'I thought we could all just *move on*, you know? Let the past stay in the past, forgive and forget. I mean, what's the point of dredging up all that old history?'

Sadie's stomach lurched. What history did she mean, was she talking about what had happened in the 1930s? Was Sadie about to find out how that story ended?

Ellie pushed her hair out of her eyes and sighed. 'See, I used to go out with Craig Mortlock.'

'You're kidding!' said Sadie. 'He was your boy-friend?' Was there anyone in this town that her mother *hadn't* gone out with?

'It was a long time ago. You know we always came up here for the holidays, and we'd hang around with Craig and the local kids. And one year, Craig and I just – clicked.' Ellie shrugged. 'He was actually pretty hot back then,' she said defensively. 'And he was a champion cricket player. Well, anyway. These things happen.'

'So...' Sadie tried not to imagine her mum and Craig Mortlock kissing. 'Why did you break up?'

'I met David,' said Ellie. 'Craig and I had been together for a couple of years. I was only eighteen. I'd let Craig decide how things were going to be; I'd sort of drifted into it. He was keener on me than I was on him, I suppose. He used to talk about me moving up here for good, living with Nana, getting a job. He'd even talked about us getting married.' Ellie snorted. 'At our age! Crazy!'

'Your Nana Jean was nineteen when she married Clarry Hazzard,' said Sadie.

Ellie stared at her. 'Was she? How do you know that?'

Sadie opened her mouth and shut it again. 'I dunno,' she said feebly. 'You must have told me.'

'Did I?' Ellie frowned. 'Well, I suppose she must have been pretty young... Anyway, as soon as I met David, I knew I didn't want to marry Craig Mortlock, no matter what a star he was at cricket, or how much land his dad owned.' Ellie fell silent.

'So, what happened?' prompted Sadie.

'Something awful,' said Ellie. 'Now I wish I hadn't started this story.'

Sadie waited.

Ellie sighed. 'One of David's mates asked him to go fishing on the lake – Lake Invergarry. But when they got there, it was a trap. Craig and some others were waiting for them. They – they beat David up. He nearly drowned.'

She was silent for a long time. Sadie stared at the floor.

At last Ellie said, 'I let David down, back then. I didn't know what to do. I thought I loved David, but I knew I'd hurt Craig. I felt guilty. I thought it was all my fault. So I ran away. I never want to be a coward like that again. I've got another chance now. I *can't* wreck it this time.'

Ellie reached for Sadie's hand and squeezed it so hard she crushed Sadie's fingers.

'Well,' said Sadie awkwardly. 'If you don't want to wreck it again, shouldn't you fix things up with David?'

Ellie laughed, and wiped her eyes. 'Yes, you're right. Where's my phone?' She stood up, went back into the kitchen and returned with her mobile in her hand, thumbing the keypad.

'Sadie,' she said. 'Better not talk about this. Not to Lachie, or Craig, or David, or Walter. There's no point stirring it all up again. Just keep it a secret, okay?'

'Okay,' agreed Sadie. Then she added, 'Anyway, I'm not talking to Lachie any more.'

But Ellie wasn't listening. She pressed the phone to her ear. 'Hi, it's me. Are you home yet? I wasn't sure you'd pick up—' She walked out of the room, and Sadie heard her bedroom door click shut.

Sadie sat on the couch. On the TV, a player was lining up a kick at goal. The umpire's whistle blew, and the ball soared into the night sky, spinning yellow against black, and the crowd roared as it sliced between the goalposts.

Sadie aimed the remote at the TV and turned everything to black.

In bed, she closed her eyes. On the other side of the wall, Ellie's voice murmured, talking to David, and the sound merged in her mind with the hum of drinkers in the pub, the roar of Lachie's trail bike, the shouts of the football crowd, the gentle tick-tick of the clock in Clarry and Jean's kitchen, and rising above them all, the long, mournful lament of the crows. *Waah... waah... waa-aah...*

And it was those cries that haunted her as she sank into a troubled sleep.

The next evening Sadie discovered that she'd lost her gloves.

'Oh, *Sadie.*' Ellie lowered her magazine. 'Not *again.*'

Sadie hovered in the doorway, waiting to see which way Ellie would go. She might say gaily, *never mind, we can pick you up another pair next time we go to Bendigo.* Or she might insist that Sadie retrace her steps for the past forty-eight hours until she found them.

'Did you lose them at school?'

'No, I had them last night when we went to the pub.'

'Did you leave them there?'

'Dunno. Can't remember. Maybe.'

Ellie raised her magazine. 'You'd better go and get them then.'

'*Now?* But it's dark!'

'I'm not made of money, you know. I can't afford to buy you new gloves every five minutes.'

'You got a new scarf,' said Sadie. '*And* a new beanie.'

'But I haven't lost them, have I?'

Sadie muttered, 'If you hadn't stayed up all night yakking to David, you wouldn't be so grumpy.'

'I beg your pardon?'

'Nothing.' Sadie dragged on her parka. 'I'm going. Probably to be *attacked* and *murdered* in the *dark*. Oh yeah, and *frozen*. Happy now?'

'Yes, thanks.' Ellie turned a page. 'I love you.'

'Weird way of showing it.'

Sadie stomped out into the twilight. A blanket of cold had settled across the plains. David had told her Boort meant 'smoke on the hill' in the local Aboriginal language. Smoke was rising now from the odd chimney in town; Sadie could taste it in the back of her throat. She shrank from the idea of walking into the pub all on her own. At least it was Sunday, a quiet night; there'd be hardly anyone there. The soft grey glow of TVs shone from the houses by the lake; in town, the main street was empty.

Wah-waah, remarked a crow from somewhere in the dusk. *Your own fault.*

'Mind your own business, stupid bird,' muttered Sadie, trudging up the hill, eyes on the pavement.

She found her gloves in the gutter outside the pub. They must have fallen from her pocket as she was struggling into her parka on the way home.

Pulling the gloves onto her icy fingers, she crossed the road and stood for a moment beneath the stern stone soldier. The old shop was closed up and empty, its windows boarded, grass sprouting from the gutters. Sadie lingered, staring. It was bizarre to think that she'd been inside that building in a different time, in a different life.

Waah...waah...

Sadie shivered, and swayed where she stood. As she put out a hand to steady herself against the memorial, a pitch-black tunnel closed around her. Wind rushed in her ears, its howling mingled with the crow's warning cry. She staggered, almost fell.

When Sadie straightened up again, she was standing by the kitchen door behind the shop, holding a tin basin in her hands. Automatically she swung her arms to fling out the washing-up water onto Mum's flower beds, shook the last drops from the basin, and wiped her damp hand on her apron.

She'd already turned to go back inside when she heard raised voices across the street outside the pub. She paused in the shadows and peered round the side of the building, knowing she couldn't be seen. She listened, her heart beating hard.

'You can't tell me what to do on my own land!' That was Mr Mortlock's voice.

'I'm tellin' you, it's wrong! It's against the Law, all the Laws, you can't do this thing; you *mustn't* do it!'

It took Sadie a moment to realise that it was Jimmy Raven shouting; Jimmy, whose voice she'd never heard raised in anger.

'How *dare* you speak to me like that?'

The dim figure of Mr Mortlock lunged forward, his hand raised to strike. But Jimmy Raven didn't flinch or step back; he stood his ground.

A door swung open and both men turned, blinking in the blaze of golden light. The door creaked shut, and a third figure, shorter than the others, joined them on the footpath.

'What's all this, then?'

A thrill of relief prickled down Sadie's back. It was Dad; he would sort this out.

'You keep out of it, Clarry,' growled Mr Mortlock.

'Come back inside and have a drink,' said Clarry. 'Too cold to stand out here arguing.' He added in a low voice, 'You get on home, Jimmy.'

'I got to speak with Mr Mortlock,' said Jimmy.

'Telling me I'm not *allowed* to dam Cross Creek!' shouted Mr Mortlock. 'Bloody cheek! *Mustn't do this, mustn't do that!* You'd think it was his own damn land!'

'Not my country. But this is my business.' Jimmy stood tall, unmoving. Mr Mortlock's bluster blew past him like a breeze past an ancient red-gum tree.

'Steady on,' said Clarry. 'No need to get excited. Jimmy, why don't you come along with me? You can have this talk another time.'

'Just because you've been to France doesn't give you licence to cheek the boss.' Mr Mortlock pointed a trembling finger at Jimmy. 'You remember that, boy. If it wasn't for me, you'd be rotting on the reserve with the rest of your miserable, god-forsaken—'

'All right, all right, Jimmy's coming along with me,' said Clarry. 'This is all a misunderstanding – things will look different in the morning, I'm sure. Good night, Gerald.'

Mr Mortlock muttered something. Then he jammed on his hat and lurched away round the corner of the pub. A moment later Sadie heard the sputter and cough of an automobile engine coming to life, and gravel sprayed as the motor roared away.

Dad led Jimmy across the street; Sadie pressed herself back into the deepest shadows by the kitchen door.

'Come inside,' Dad urged Jimmy.

'No, I got to get home.'

There was a pause. Clarry said, 'Are you going to tell me what this is all about, Bird?'

Sadie had never heard Dad use Jimmy's army nickname.

Jimmy shook his head. 'He wants to flood the valley.' His voice was deep with despair.

'Well, it is his land, Jimmy,' said Clarry. 'Why shouldn't he build a dam if he wants to? For heaven's sake, some of his own family are buried in that valley. If he doesn't mind covering their graves with water, why should you worry about it?'

'No!' Jimmy broke away; Sadie could see the fierce light in his eyes. 'No. He mustn't do that.'

'Jimmy, be reasonable—'

'It's like – it'd be like me settin' that church on fire.' Jimmy flung out his arm in the direction of the little weatherboard church. 'What would you say if I set the church on fire, hey?'

'Jimmy!' Dad's voice was shocked. 'You can't let people hear you talk like that!'

Sadie clutched at the tin basin's rim. The new church, with the bell that everyone had scrimped to pay for, and the coloured glass in the windows. God's own house, a sacred place. The thought of anyone burning it down filled her with a sick horror.

'That's how it is for my people,' said Jimmy in a low voice. 'The same thing. That place was a meeting place for our people, a holy place. You seen them trees there? They're special trees, a special place. You understand?'

Clarry was silent. At last he said, 'No, Jimmy. It's not the same, not for me. I'm sorry, but...'

His voice trailed away, and the two men stood without speaking. All around them, the darkness was alive with the tiny noises of the night: the scamper and rustle of small animals, the sigh and whisper of stirring leaves, the distant creak of ancient trees.

Clarry shook his head and lifted his hand in a gesture of regret or bewilderment or helplessness. Then he turned and let himself into the kitchen; the door groaned and banged behind him.

Sadie whispered, 'Jimmy?'

Jimmy searched for her in the shadows and gave her a sad smile. 'I thought I seen you there, hidin' in the dark.'

'What you were telling Dad just now – I think I understand.'

'You think so?' Jimmy shook his head. 'You understand it? Maybe you can explain it all to me some time.' He was silent for a moment. 'You know, Sadie, this isn't my country. I wasn't born here; this isn't my land. My country is way down south by the sea. I don't belong in this place. I don't reckon I'll ever see my country again. But I know a special place when I see it. There's a special place in that valley. I know it. The people who belong to that place, they're not here to protect it, so I got to do it. You understand that? That's what I got to do. He builds that dam, drowns that place, I don't know what might happen. Bad things. I don't know what. I been trying to tell him, but he won't listen. Even your dad don't understand. Gerry Mortlock never going to listen.'

'It's not your fault,' said Sadie. 'You've done your best.'

'Law's the Law,' said Jimmy. 'Law's broken, we all suffer. I gotta do something.'

Sadie bit her lip. 'If I can help,' she said. 'If you can think of anything—'

'Too late for that, Sadie, I reckon.' Jimmy nodded toward the door. 'You go in. Your mum'll be wanting you.'

Sadie glanced back at the house and then back to Jimmy. But he was gone.

Sadie was alone in the darkness, the washing basin cold in her fingers; the stars prickling icy overhead in the vault of the sky; a wild cawing in her ears, and a bright light dazzling her eyes...

She was on her hands and knees in the road, blinded by car headlights.

'You bloody little idiot!' someone shouted. 'I could have killed you!'

Sadie scrambled to her feet, waved her gloves at the car in a dumbstruck apology, and staggered off into the night. She told herself that it was fright at being nearly run over that made her legs wobble.

But a sick feeling of dread churned in her stomach, a foreboding that something terrible was going to happen. Blinded by the car's lights, Sadie stretched out her hands in the soupy dark, as if she could grope from one fistful of shadow to the next. The night thrummed with rustlings and scamperings and the slow whir of insects, but she couldn't see.

S adie dreamed.

In the dream, she walked across an endless plain. It was night. The ground beneath her feet was swallowed in darkness, but the sky that arched over her shimmered with innumerable stars. She walked, stumbling over stones, toward the sound of weeping.

A crow, larger and blacker than any crow she'd ever seen, lifted his head as she approached, as if he had been waiting for her. Tears etched a terrible silver trail from each of his bright eyes. He didn't speak but gazed at her from a grief so deep there were no words.

She wanted to comfort him, but she didn't know how. In her dream, she clumsily reached an arm across the crow's neck. But as she tried to embrace him, he shivered and dissolved, evaporating beneath her touch, and her arm plunged into nothingness, through dark as soft as feathers. There was only the sorrow-struck cry, *waa-aah... waa-aah...* that echoed across the earth, inside her head, vibrating through her bones, and she trembled awake in her own bed.

On Saturday, she didn't go with David and Ellie to watch the Magpies lose to St Arnaud. Ellie didn't try to persuade her to come; her mum seemed more than happy to seize the chance of some time alone with David to finish making up after their argument.

Sadie finished her homework in record time and slouched around the house feeling bored. She thought about visiting the stones, but her dream had made her uneasy. She was worried that the crows might be angry that she'd shown their place to Lachie; maybe it was best to stay away.

After a day of boredom, she eagerly agreed to go to the pub for dinner.

Ellie caught her in the bathroom. 'I think it'll be all right tonight,' she said in a low voice. 'They just needed to get used to the idea. Lots of people saw us at the footy today, and no one said anything.' She glanced at herself in the mirror, touched up her lipstick and practised a quick smile. 'It'll be fine. You'll see.'

Sadie wondered how her mum could possibly know if anyone had said anything or not, but she kept quiet.

As they walked to the pub, David asked Sadie how she liked living in the country.

'I hated it at first,' said Sadie. 'But I like it more now.'

'Yeah? What do you like?'

'Well...' Sadie considered. 'The stars are kind of beautiful. And I like that sculpture made out of old spanners. That's cool.'

'Gotta love the spanners,' David laughed; he seemed to find Sadie funny, even when she didn't mean to be, but his wide smile was so infectious that she couldn't mind.

'Where's Walter?' she asked.

David tipped his head to look at her. 'At his aunties'.'

Sadie thought that David and Ellie exchanged a glance over the top of her head. Annoyed, she stalked ahead.

They found a table in the dining room. Sadie's heart flopped over when Craig and Amanda Mortlock took the table beside them, with Lachie and an older blonde girl she hadn't seen before. Craig leaned across to introduce his daughter Bethany. 'She's down at uni,' he said proudly. 'Must be smarter than her old man, I only lasted two terms!'

Bethany looked smooth and bored, like her mother. They talked to each other in low voices, ignoring Ellie and David and Sadie. Sadie could see Lachie trying to catch her eye, but she refused to look at him. She wished more than ever that she'd never shown him the stones.

Toward the end of dinner, Sadie heard Craig say to Lachie, 'If we don't start winning games, we're looking at a merger. Maybe not next year, but the year after for sure. No one wants to play for a losing team. Damn shame to see the club disappear after a hundred and twenty-odd years.'

'We need a new coach,' said Lachie. 'Sorry, Dad, but it's true. Vic's useless.'

Ellie leaned over and rapped her spoon on the table to catch Craig's attention. 'You looking for a coach for the Magpies?'

'We could use someone to help Vic out,' admitted Craig. 'He was great, twenty years ago, but he's a bit past it now.'

Ellie smiled. 'David can coach.'

'Is that right?' Craig shifted in his chair and stared at David.

David shot Ellie a frowning glance. 'Used to coach in Mildura,' he said reluctantly. 'But that was a long time ago.'

'Produced some great players, your lot.' Craig swigged his beer. 'Bloody geniuses, some of them.'

'I'm not that good,' said David.

'Can't take discipline, though, that's the trouble,' said Craig. 'Brains aren't wired up that way. Brilliant, quick, amazing skills, but unreliable. Can't turn up to training week in, week out. No commitment, no discipline.'

David said, 'I had enough discipline to make it all the way through a uni degree.'

His eyes and Craig's locked for a moment.

'I had family problems.' Craig's jaw jutted out. 'My father died unexpectedly. I had to come home and run the farm.'

'Had some unexpected deaths in my family, too,' said David. 'Brothers, cousins.'

Craig shifted uncomfortably in his chair. 'What I said – no need to take it personally.'

'I didn't.'

Craig set down his beer and leaned forward. 'Talking of family, how's your nephew settling in?'

'You mean Walter? Fine, thanks.'

'Yeah? Only I heard he's making it tough for himself. Telling lies, picking fights, making trouble ...Won't make friends that way, not round here.'

Ellie's eyes flashed. 'Walter's a great kid. If anyone's been picking fights, you can bet it's not him.'

Craig said blandly, 'Just telling you what I've heard. My mistake.'

Lachie ducked his head and scratched the back of his neck.

'He's come here to make a fresh start,' said Ellie loudly. 'It's a shame some people won't let him do that.'

'Ellie. Let it go,' David murmured.

Ellie laid down her knife and fork. 'Isn't it *interesting* how black boys *make trouble*, but white boys just *have accidents?*'

Craig's face flushed purple. 'Beg your pardon?'

'You know exactly what I'm talking about! When someone *made trouble* at your lake by almost drowning, because someone else had *accidentally* punched him in the face!'

'Well, maybe *someone else* should have thought twice before she ran off with a new boyfriend!' shouted Craig.

'Well, maybe if her old boyfriend hadn't been such a dickhead, she wouldn't have had to!' shouted Ellie.

'*What?*' said Bethany.

Amanda's face was white as soap. The whole dining room was hushed; everyone was pretending not to listen.

'Sorry,' said Ellie, into the silence. 'I apologise. That was totally unnecessary. Sorry.'

Craig gave a forced laugh. 'Jeez, you start out with a nice polite chat about football and look what happens.'

David pushed back his chair. 'Time we were leaving, I reckon.'

Ellie groped her arms into her coat. 'Bye, Amanda. Nice to meet you, Bethany. See you, Lachie. Sorry, Craig.'

'Don't worry about it,' said Craig. Sadie thought he looked oddly satisfied.

Bethany's bewildered voice followed them as they pushed toward the front bar. 'What was *that* all about?'

Ellie's face was pink. She said to Sadie, 'Wait outside with David. I'll pay.'

'No, I'll pay,' said David, and pushed ahead of Ellie to the till. Sadie glimpsed his face and it scared her; she'd never seen it look so hard and grim.

As soon as they all were outside in the cold, David said, 'Well, at least I won't have to coach the bloody Boort football team.'

'Why shouldn't you coach them? Forget about Craig. The rest of them are good kids, they deserve a decent coach.'

'I'd rather spend my energy on kids who really need it.'

Ellie thrust her hands into her gloves. 'You mean not white kids?'

'That's not what I said—'

The pub door burst open and Lachie Mortlock hurtled out like a rocket. 'Good, I caught you!' He had no coat on, and his cheeks flushed in the chilly air. 'David, Dad said to tell you he's sorry if he said anything that offended you. He said it's all water under the bridge. And if you did want to give us a hand with the coaching, he'd make it worth your while.'

'Oh, really?' said Ellie, switching sides again. 'Well, you tell him—'

David interrupted. 'Tell him it's okay. I'm sorry, too.'

Lachie shifted from foot to foot and rubbed his nose. 'You know…we could really do with a new coach. Or someone to help out, at least.' He looked pleadingly at David. 'Training's on Thursday nights at the oval. If you're not busy.'

David looked up at the sky. 'I'll think about it. I guess you've gotta start building bridges some-where.'

'David!' Ellie threw her arms around him.

Sadie looked away, embarrassed, and saw Lachie watching her. He blurted out, 'Sadie, you want to stay? The pool comp's on tonight. Want to be my partner?'

A week ago, Sadie would have given anything to hear those words from Lachie's lips, but now she silently shook her head. Then she realised that no one had seen it in the near dark between the street lights; they thought she was hesitating.

'I'll walk her home afterwards, Ellie, I promise,' said Lachie. 'It won't be too late, we'll finish up before eleven.'

'How about it, Sadie?' said Ellie. 'Sounds like fun.'

Sadie opened her mouth to say, *no thanks*. Then it occurred to her that Ellie probably wanted to snuggle up on the couch with David without her hanging around.

'Okay,' she muttered. 'I'll stay.' She hoped her mother would be grateful.

'Cool,' said Lachie. 'See you on Thursday, David? Hopefully?'

'Maybe,' said David. 'No promises.'

'Let's go,' said Lachie. He put his hand on Sadie's back and guided her back inside the pub. Despite herself, Sadie felt a thrill run down her spine.

S adie had to force herself to walk soberly home beside Lachie in the dark; she felt like skipping along the lake-shore road and shouting to the moon, *We won! We won!* Giggles fizzed inside her as she remembered the looks of startled respect on Troy and Hammer's faces. Nank had given her a hug that smelled of aftershave, and Jules had said, *Not bad, kiddo.* They'd even found her a beer. She'd sipped it, but it tasted so bitter she was glad to pass it on to Lachie.

And now she was walking home *by moonlight*, with Lachie Mortlock, *alone.* For once she wished the distance between the pub and her house was longer.

'I don't want you to think Dad's a bad person,' said Lachie suddenly. 'Cos he's not.'

'Huh?' Sadie had forgotten the argument at

dinner; now a glass of icy water seemed to drench her insides. 'Oh. Right, yeah.'

'He's just old-school, you know? He doesn't *know* any blackfellas.'

Sadie could hear the earnestness in Lachie's voice. But the way he said *blackfellas* made her uneasy. That was a word David and Walter used about themselves, but it didn't sound right when Lachie said it.

The joy and triumph of the competition curdled inside her. 'I didn't notice you sticking up for Walter and me last week when everyone was kicking us off the pool table.'

'That wasn't about Walter being black. You guys pushed in; it wasn't your *turn*. Come on, cut me some slack. I couldn't back down in front of the guys; I would've looked like a wuss.'

She wanted to forgive him. She wanted to believe in Lachie. And some secret sweetness lay in the fact that he was trying to persuade her. He actually cared what she thought.

'Okay,' she said, as they reached her driveway. 'And I'm sorry my mum called your dad a dickhead.'

Lachie laughed. 'That's cool. Don't worry about it.' He flashed her his best shy smile. 'This is your place, yeah?'

'This is it.'

'Okay. See ya.'

Lachie flipped a casual hand, spun round and walked back along the road. Sadie stared after him, trying to swallow her disappointment. *You didn't think he was going to* kiss *you, did you?* she told herself savagely. *You moron, you're only fourteen... nearly fourteen... he must be sixteen at least...* But she couldn't help lingering, listening to the crisp crunch of his shoes on the gravel fade into the large watchful quiet of the night.

She turned and headed for the house. Mum had promised to leave the back door unlocked.

A shape reared into her face, separating itself from the darkness.

Sadie screamed, but her mouth was choked with feathers, and no sound came out. Her heart banged wildly against her ribs.

Wah? Wah? came a soft query. *Is it you?*

And she knew it was a crow, this piece of darkness. She could make out the dim outline of wings, sharp feathers tucked into its side, and when it turned its head, she saw the gleam of its beak in the moonlight. Her heart was pounding. What was it doing here? How had it found her in her own backyard? This wasn't the crows' place; they belonged to the stone circle and the dried lake.

As if it had read her mind, the crow spoke. 'All of this country is crow country.'

Sadie nodded dumbly. There was a rustle of feathers as the crow rearranged its wings.

'Why have you not kept Crow's secret?' it said.

Sadie pressed her hands together. 'I know, I'm sorry, I shouldn't have shown Lachie your special place. I didn't mean to; it just happened... And he might have found it anyway; it's on his land...'

'*His* land?' mocked the crow. '*Waah!*'

'I'm sorry,' Sadie whispered again. She was afraid. She wondered if she could sneak past, make a run for the safety of the house. She edged sideways, but the crow made an abrupt movement and she froze.

'Tell the story.'

'W-what?'

'*Wah-wah-waaah!*' The crow's voice creaked impatiently through the dark. 'You see what Crow cannot see. Crow wants the story.'

'What story?' Sadie was bewildered.

'*Waah!* The story that belongs to you. You see what is hidden from Crow. Crow knows wrongs were done, but Crow cannot see. You must tell; you must do what is needed; you must finish what is left undone. It is the Law.'

'I don't understand!' cried Sadie. 'What do you want me to do? I don't know what you want!'

'*Wah!*' The crow reared up angrily, wings out-stretched, and Sadie shrank back. 'Do you have no Law? When a man is killed, the death must be punished. When precious things are stolen they must be returned. Are you an infant? Do you know nothing? Tell the story; tell Crow what you see!'

'I don't *know* what I see!' cried Sadie wretchedly. Her breath was a white cloud in the cold night. 'Do you mean Clarry? Or is it something to do with Jimmy Raven? Is that what you wanted me to see? He had a fight – he said – he said—' She struggled to remember what Jimmy had told her in the darkness. 'Something precious was going to be destroyed. Is that it? Tell me!'

'*You* must tell! You ask too many questions. *Wah!* You have no respect!'

'But—' Sadie stopped herself just in time.

There was a long silence. Only the rustle of feathers and the soft click of a beak told her that the crow was still there, waiting. Sadie shivered. She felt stupid and sleepy and bewildered.

At last she heard the crow's low, creaking voice. 'You must finish the story. That is what is important.'

'But how can I?' said Sadie in a small voice. 'What's happened has happened. The past is past; it's gone; it's over.'

'No, no,' said the crow softly. 'The past is never over; it is never lost. It circles, as the stones circle, as the stars circle, as the earth circles. The story tells itself again, memory and story and land and Law. The stones are spilled; the tears are spilled; the blood is spilled; the Law is broken. The Law is broken!' the crow cried with sudden violence, and Sadie leapt back as the bird reared up and beat its wings against the sky, as if pieces of thunder clashed together. 'When the Law is broken there must be punishment! This story belongs to you. You must do what Crow cannot do; go into the shadows where Crow cannot go!'

'I don't understand!' cried Sadie in terror.

But the crow was gone, and Sadie was shouting to an empty yard, her words spiralling away, dissolving in white mist.

'Sadie?' called Ellie sharply from the back door. 'Is Lachie with you? What's going on?'

Sadie gazed around despairingly, but there was nothing to see except the wires of the clothesline strung across the sky, the silvery shadows, the shaggy limbs of the old mallee gum stirring in the breeze, whispering a secret she couldn't understand.

'Are you sure you're all right?' Ellie laid her hand on Sadie's forehead. 'You haven't been yourself all week.'

It was true; Sadie had been feeling oddly disconnected from her own life. School, Mum, Boort, even Lachie, who'd smiled at her twice at school that week – none of it seemed quite real. She felt as if she were floating through a dream, watching herself from a distance.

Only the crows seemed real, as vividly real as three-dimensional figures moving against a flat painted backdrop. The words the crow had spoken burned into Sadie's memory. *When the Law is broken there must be punishment!* Night after night she woke, struggling to free herself from dreams in which she was searching, or running, or screaming out. In the dreams, she didn't know what she was hunting for, or fleeing from, or what made her cry out. Only the sense of panic remained, knotted always in her stomach.

Even the crows at school had changed. There had always been clouds of them, rising and falling on the oval and the netball court, flapping and squawking over the rubbish bins, perched on the gutters as they exchanged their melancholy cries. But now they'd begun to follow Sadie about, hopping along behind as if they were imitating her, mocking her. They were always watching, heads cocked, their bright eyes fixed on her, and their remarks were a running commentary on her every movement. Sadie knew it, even if no one else could understand them. *Waah? Waa-aah! There she is. What's she doing now? She's drinking water. Here she comes. Crow has chosen her. Crow has tricked her. Wah! That's Crow's secret!*

Sadie shifted under Ellie's hand. 'I'm okay.'

'Do you want to stay home from school? The art show's tonight, remember; it'll be a long day. We could skip it if you like.'

'No, I'd rather go.' Would Lachie be there? He wasn't really the arty type.

Ellie smiled. 'David's coming, too. Did you know Walter's got a piece in the show?'

'Has he?'

'David's working in Bendigo today. He said he might bring home some Chinese takeaway, for a treat, and we can eat at their place. If you feel up to it.'

'Okay.' Sadie swung her legs out of bed. She asked casually, 'So, will we be staying over?' David had stayed at their place last Saturday night for the first time.

Ellie hesitated. 'David doesn't think that's a good idea. Not for the moment. He's not sure if Walter's ready.'

And what about if I'm ready? thought Sadie. *You didn't bother to ask how I feel about it.* Though, in fact, she didn't mind.

'Anyway, it's not as – convenient – for us to stay at David's. He often has family staying over, extra people in the house. You know.'

Sadie grabbed her uniform.

Ellie perched on the edge of the bed watching her. 'David went to footy training last night,' she said.

'Oh! I didn't think he would.'

'Well, he did.'

'That's good. It's good, isn't it?'

'Of course it is. It's good for everyone. It shows we can put the past behind us, move on, forget all that—' Ellie waved a hand. 'All that unpleasantness.'

'Yes,' said Sadie. 'I guess.'

Ellie looked annoyed. 'Well, I think David's very brave. Good on him!'

'Good on him,' echoed Sadie.

But the anxious knot stayed tied in her stomach. Sadie wasn't sure that the past could be so easily forgotten.

The artworks were hung around the walls of the community centre that stood between the high school and the sports ground. Parents and students eddied slowly, a hum of conversation rising to fill the cavernous space.

'Is this your painting, Walter?' Ellie stared at the label beside it.

'You sound surprised.' David grinned at her. 'What did you expect, a dot painting?'

'No, I – oh, shut up.' Ellie gave him a playful push. 'It's really good, that's all. It's great, Walter. I didn't know you were such an artist.'

'Thanks,' mumbled Walter.

Sadie gazed at the portrait of the old Aboriginal woman. She had a deeply wrinkled face and wispy white hair. But her eyes were deep and dark, unfathomable.

'Is she your grandmother?' asked Ellie.

Walter shook his head. 'Auntie Lily. She lives here in Boort too.'

'It's wonderful,' said Ellie. 'Will you paint me?'

'Sure,' said Walter, struggling to hide his dismay. Ellie laughed.

'She's only teasing,' said Sadie. She leaned forward, peering at a detail in Walter's painting. An electric shock fizzed through her. In the background, perched on a fence, Walter had painted a black bird.

Sadie pointed. 'Is that – is that a crow?'

'Yeah. That's Auntie Lily's totem.'

'Oh.' Sadie wasn't sure what that meant, but she was too shy to ask.

Ellie wasn't shy. 'What's that, Walter? What's *your* totem? What's yours, David? Can you choose your own?'

Walter said, 'Auntie Lily doesn't like me talking about that stuff too much.'

David shook his head. 'You spend too much time with Auntie Lily.'

Walter opened his mouth to argue, but just then a voice rang out across the hall.

'Dave! Davo!'

Craig Mortlock waved as he strode toward them. Amanda was nowhere in sight. Craig grinned and slapped David on the shoulder.

'Great session last night! You certainly showed those boys a trick or two. Very impressive, Davo. No promises, obviously, but if the boys pick up the way they did last night, and the season improves…well, you might be looking at a permanent position.'

'I'm only there to give Vic a hand,' said David. 'I'm not trying to put anyone out of a job.' He saw Lachie standing behind his father. 'Sorry you missed out on the team this time, mate. Maybe next week.'

'Yeah,' said Lachie.

'Hi, Lachie,' said Sadie breathlessly.

'Hi, Sadie.' Lachie threw her a half-smile.

Sadie beamed back foolishly, and couldn't think of anything else to say.

'That is *so* exciting about the coaching!' said Ellie, as they gathered round the table in David's kitchen, helping themselves to reheated Chinese takeaway. 'Did you hear what Craig said? A permanent position! That means they'll sack Vic, for sure. Craig's the president; what he says goes, and if he wants you, you've got the job.'

'Hold on, who says I want the job?' David was half-laughing, half-cross. 'I don't mind going down the oval once in a while to help them with their handballing, but I've got no plans to be the Boort football coach.'

'Oh, David, why not?'

'I told you, I've got better things to do.' He

squeezed her hand. 'Like spending time with you, for instance.'

Walter and Sadie rolled their eyes.

'I'm prepared to make the sacrifice,' said Ellie.

'Really? Why?'

'*Because* – I want us to fit in. As a couple. I want us to be a part of the community.'

'Well, I'm not sure if I do.' David released Ellie's hand and dug his chopsticks into the lemon chicken.

'David—'

'Let's talk about it later.'

Ellie leaned across the table. 'So, Walter, what about these totems, then?'

'Maybe David should explain it.'

David shrugged. 'You know more about it than me, mate. You're the one who spends hours talking to Auntie Lily when you should be doing your homework.'

'It's important,' said Walter.

'Of course it is!' said Ellie. 'Walter needs to know about his culture.'

'Yeah,' said David. 'But there's no point knowing about your culture if you can't get a job.'

'You can do both, surely,' said Ellie. 'Tell me, Walter, I'm interested.'

'Well…' said Walter slowly. 'Some of the stuff

Auntie Lily tells me, it's secret, okay? But you've heard of the Dreaming, right?'

Ellie nodded. Walter's dark gaze sought out Sadie, and she nodded too.

'For our people, the land was created long ago, in the time of the Dreaming, when the ancestral spirits moved across the country. They made the hills and the rivers, the swamps and the waterholes. That's why our spirit ancestors are so important. They make the land, and the land belongs to them, and they make us, too.'

Sadie's heart was thumping. 'Who – who are they?'

'Well, round this country, everything belongs to Bunjil the Eaglehawk, or Waa the Crow.'

Walter was gazing levelly at Sadie. Sadie stared back at him. Neither of them moved.

'The crow's name is Waa?' Ellie was saying. 'I love it! Just like the noise they make!'

'You all right there, Sadie?' said David.

Sadie looked down, and took a deep breath. 'I guess – there are lots of crows round here.'

'Sure are.' David balanced a dumpling on his chopsticks. 'I heard one of the creeks round here used to be called Crow Creek. But they call it Cross Creek now.'

'Why did they change it?' said Sadie.

Walter said, 'Some whitefellas think crows are unlucky.'

'Ridiculous!' snorted Ellie.

Sadie said, 'Why?'

'Crows are supposed to foretell death in lots of European cultures. In North America, too, I think,' said David.

'Not for us. For our people, that's owls or curlews,' said Walter.

'There's a church next to Cross Creek, isn't there? Maybe they changed the name when they built it,' said Ellie. 'When they laid down their religion on top of yours, they changed the crow to a cross. Fascinating.'

'And now there's more people at the footy on a Saturday afternoon than go to church on a Sunday morning,' said David. 'We should be talking about how Boort's going to whip Birchip Watchem tomorrow.'

'Better get your protein up, Mr Assistant Coach,' said Ellie. 'Here, try the beef.'

Walter was still watching Sadie. He said in a low voice, 'Our people lived in this country for forty thousand years, maybe more. No other culture in the history of the world's lasted that long. The Egyptians, the Greeks, the Romans – they all destroyed themselves. Not us. Because we knew how to live *with* the land, not fight it. So we survived.'

Ellie said, 'Till the whitefellas came.'

Walter looked at her. 'We're still surviving.'

'Yes, of course.' Flustered, Ellie dropped a piece of chicken. 'Of course you are ...'

'Don't know about Bunjil and Waa, though,' said David. 'Don't reckon they made it.'

'Oh, no!' cried Sadie. 'They did! I know they did!'

Ellie and David burst out laughing. 'All right, darling.' Ellie patted her hand. 'I'm sure Bungee and Waa appreciate you believing in them, even if no one else does.'

Sadie stared down into her bowl. She didn't dare glance at Walter. But she could feel his dark eyes burning into her, not blinking, not looking away.

16

To everyone's amazement, Boort did defeat Birchip Watchem the next day. The big forward, Muz, kicked a goal after the final siren to snatch victory for the Magpies, and the black-and-white spectators round the Birchip oval erupted into cheers of delirious joy. Sadie clapped until her hands hurt. Ellie grabbed David in a wild hug.

'It was the handballs – it's all about the handballs!' she shouted gleefully.

'Well—' David ducked his head and grinned. 'There's more to it than handballing.'

The players were spilling off the ground. Many of them paused to thump David on the back. Ellie whooped and applauded; Walter stuck his fingers in his mouth and whistled.

'Go, Magpies!' shouted Sadie.

Out of the corner of her eye, she saw a crow hop to the rim of an overflowing rubbish bin. *No offence*, she said hastily, silently, in its direction. It bowed gravely, fixed one gleaming eye on her, and winked.

'Thanks for the help, mate.'

'Good on ya, mate.'

'No worries,' said David, shaking hands with one player after another.

Walter murmured to Sadie, 'You'd think they'd won the final.'

'Anything's possible!' roared Craig Mortlock behind them. 'What a game, eh? If we keep playing like that, who knows?' He flung his arm round David. 'Glad I caught you, mate. Something I want to ask your advice about.'

'Yeah, what's that?' said David, distracted.

Craig leaned into David's face and lowered his voice. 'Found something very interesting on my land. Aboriginal artefacts. Wondered if you could tell me what they'd be worth.'

Sadie's heart stood still. Walter hadn't heard. He touched Sadie's sleeve. 'Is that Mr Harris from school over there?'

'Ssh!' said Sadie frantically.

David was saying, 'What kind of artefacts?'

'Artwork, Aboriginal artwork.'

'You mean rock paintings?'

'Something like that.'

David frowned. 'Well, I don't know much about that stuff. But if it's rock art, I don't see how you could sell it. If it's in a cave——'

'Not in a cave.'

'So where is it?'

'On my land,' said Craig, clearly reluctant to give away any more details. He chewed his lip. 'So you reckon it'd be worth checking out a museum, a university, somewhere like that? There are people who collect this stuff, right? Must be worth *something*. And I've got some other bits and pieces lying around, reckon I should dig them out too?'

Someone was trying to give David a can of beer; he waved it away. 'Listen, mate, it's a difficult area. If it's a cultural site, it'll be protected. You can't just hack out bits of rock art and sell them off; it's against the law.'

'Sacred site, you reckon? Everything's a bloody sacred site these days. Every time a farmer wants to cut down a tree or build a dam or make a bit of money, there's some bloody government official standing in his way with a piece of paper saying no!'

'Hardly,' said Ellie. 'Be fair, Craig; that's not true.'

'Whole bloody country's a sacred site, according to some of his lot,' growled Craig.

Ellie began to protest, but Walter cut in. 'That's right. Whole country *is* sacred. Needs respect.'

Craig shot him a scornful look. 'You want to watch what you say, son. Doesn't bother me if you shoot your mouth off, but I'm just telling you there are some people round here who don't appreciate that kind of talk—'

'And there's plenty more who'd agree with him,' said David calmly. 'We got to protect our heritage.'

'No point protecting it if no one ever sees it, is there? Put it in the museum, everyone gets the benefit, right?'

'You can't move stuff from where it belongs,' said Walter. 'That's not right.'

Someone yelled from a car window, 'See you at the pub, Morty? See you at the pub, Davo?'

Both men raised an arm in salute, and Ellie yelled back, 'See you there!'

David turned back to Craig. 'How about you let me look at whatever it is you've found, then we can talk about what to do next?'

Craig chortled. 'Oh, no, no, no, mate, you're not getting me like that! No, this stays in the family; know what I mean?'

David shrugged. 'Up to you, mate. Let me know if you change your mind.'

'Will do, mate, will do. Great work with the boys; did I say that? See you at the pub, Ellie?' Craig winked at them all and barged off through the crowd.

'What was all *that* about?' said Ellie.

But Sadie was already racing to the pavilion, burrowing between backs, hardly aware of Walter at her heels. Lachie was standing by his trail bike with the rest of the gang around him. Sadie stormed up.

'You told your dad!'

'What?' Lachie frowned down at her.

'You know what I'm talking about!' Hot tears stung behind Sadie's eyes. 'That was our secret!'

Jules drew back on a cigarette. 'Bit young for you, isn't she, Lock?'

'*Oo-ooh!*' sang Hammer. 'Lachie's got a girlfriend!'

Lachie scowled. 'Shut your face.'

'You promised it would be our secret!'

Lachie put his face close to Sadie's. 'How could it be a secret? It's on our land.'

'But I found it!' said Sadie.

'But it's not yours,' said Lachie.

'It's not yours either.'

Lachie laughed, more puzzled than angry. 'If it's not mine, I don't know whose it is. My family's owned that lake and the valley and all the land around it for a hundred and fifty years.'

'But—'

'But nothing. Now be a good kid and get lost, will you? You're making a goose of yourself.' He surveyed

Sadie's hot, angry face, and gave her shoulder a little shake. 'See you back at the pub, yeah? I'll give you a game of pool,' he said, not unkindly, then turned his back, dismissing her.

Walter touched Sadie's arm. 'Come on. Your mum's calling.'

Sadie smudged the tears from her face before Ellie or David could see. Walter glanced at her as she stumbled toward the car, but he didn't say anything.

Behind the toilet block, Sadie stopped. 'Why did you say that to Craig, about the whole country being sacred? That's not true, is it?'

'Kind of. Like Auntie Lily says. The whole land is made by the ancestors, so it's all sacred. But some places are more special than others.'

He gave her a quick look, and for a moment Sadie was tempted to tell him everything. Didn't Walter deserve to know about the stones, more than Craig Mortlock did? But there wasn't time: Ellie was scanning the crowd, hands on hips, her face screwed up in exasperation.

A crow cried from the roof of the toilet block. *Waah... waah... Be careful, girl...*

Sadie gave her eyes a final swipe. 'Come on,' she said. 'Let's go.'

'**D**amn!' muttered Ellie, her head in the fridge. 'I thought we had bacon. Sadie, could you run over to the supermarket? There's just time before it shuts.'

Reluctantly, because it was growing dark outside, Sadie shrugged on her parka and grabbed Ellie's wallet from the kitchen bench. 'Just bacon?'

'Pick up some milk while you're there – oh, and a potato... And if you feel like some chocolate after dinner...'

Sadie sighed heavily and turned back for a shopping bag.

'Thank you!' called Ellie.

'That's okay!' Sadie yelled from the door. *Wow,* she thought, *when did we start being so nice to each other?*

The chilly twilight air slapped her awake. Clouds scudded across the sky as she hurried along the road. She had five minutes till the store closed.

The automatic doors slid open, and she darted inside. Behind the register, a pinch-faced woman with sandy hair glanced up from her magazine. She was Fox's mum, Sadie knew. Fox himself lounged across the checkout, waiting for his mother to finish work, picking at his fingernails. Mrs Fox nodded briefly at Sadie, then returned her attention to the celebrity gossip.

Sadie found milk, chocolate and bacon, but there were no potatoes in the vegetable section. She hesitated, but she knew that Ellie would say, *just ask!*

Sadie stepped toward the checkout and cleared her throat. 'Excuse me...'

Without warning, the supermarket whirled about her. Sadie clutched at the chip rack, and found herself grabbing at empty air. The checkouts dissolved, the fridge and the shelves of tins faded to shadows. A long counter formed itself along one wall, shelves banked up behind it, barrels and boxes crowded around Sadie's legs. Instead of the sharp face of Mrs Fox, Sadie saw her mother, Jean – forehead creased, lips moving silently as she counted out pennies from the till. The modern supermarket was gone; she as standing in the old shop across the road, the Hazzards' shop.

'You can lock up now, love,' said her mother, sweeping the pennies into her hand, and Sadie flipped the sign on the door to CLOSED and pulled down the blind. She had her hand on the bolt when the door was pushed violently open, almost knocking her down.

Mr Mortlock staggered in, panting, wild-eyed. He was covered in blood.

'Jean!' he gasped. 'Jean—'

The colour drained from her mother's face. 'What's happened?' she cried.

Gerald Mortlock shook his head. 'I'm not hurt – I—' He staggered forward and Sadie thought he would fall.

Her mother said fiercely, 'Bolt the door, Sadie!'

Sadie sprang to shoot the bolt across. Blood dripped onto the worn floorboards, small bright splatters of crimson.

'What have you done?' whispered Jean. 'God help you, what have you done?'

Mr Mortlock reached out a hand to steady himself, and Sadie recoiled as his blood-stained fingers touched the shelves. *We'll have to clean it; who's going to clean up all this mess?* she thought.

'Clarry—' he began.

'You've not hurt Clarry!' cried Jean, her eyes like holes burned in a white cloth. 'Oh, dear God, no!'

'No! Not Clarry,' said Mr Mortlock thickly. 'But I need him – need his help – need...' He lurched and slid down the counter to the floor.

'Sadie, fetch your dad,' said Jean. 'Quickly!'

Sadie froze, and then she was stumbling behind the counter, through the door into the house, pushing the little ones aside. 'Where's Mum? I hurt my finger,' whined Betty. Philip was howling somewhere.

'Stay here!' hissed Sadie urgently. 'And be quiet!'

Betty began a wail of protest.

'Oh, shut up, do!' cried Sadie. 'Go and find John – Where's Dad?'

Betty pointed outside, sobbing; and then, mercifully, Clarry appeared in the doorway in his shirt-sleeves and braces, folding the newspaper with his square capable hands. Sadie threw herself at him.

'Come quick!'

She dragged him through the house into the shop and slammed the connecting door in Betty's outraged face.

Mr Mortlock was slumped on the floor, a scarecrow without stuffing. Mum knelt beside him, holding a tin mug of water; but he batted it aside without looking. Mum scrambled up as Dad came in.

'He won't tell me. Oh, Clarry—'

'Get back to the kids,' said Dad. 'Don't frighten them. I'll take care of this.'

Mum twisted her hands in her pinny, her eyes big with dread. 'Clarry—'

'It's all right, Jean. I'll take care of it,' said Dad firmly, and Mum edged back behind the counter and slipped into the house. Sadie started to follow, but Dad put out a hand to stop her. 'Might need you, love.'

Sadie nodded dumbly, half-terrified, half-proud that Dad trusted her.

Dad crouched on the floor. 'It's all right, mate,' he said quietly. 'Whatever's happened—'

Mr Mortlock's hand shot out and twisted into Dad's shirt. 'I've killed the bugger, Clarry. I've gone and killed him.'

'Settle down, Gerry.' Dad's voice was firm and soothing, the same voice he used when Betty was fussing about a skinned knee. 'You can bet your boots you haven't killed anybody.'

'So help me God, Lofty,' said Mr Mortlock hoarsely. 'I didn't mean it, but I've killed him.'

Sadie was frozen, terrified, her heart pumping a mile a minute.

Dad said, 'Who, Gerry?'

'Jimmy Raven!' It was an anguished howl.

Sadie sucked in her breath, and stuffed her knuckles into her mouth to stifle a moan.

Dad straightened up sharply. 'Where is he?'

'Down by Cross Creek, round the back of the old graveyard. There's a ring of stones...'

'I know the place,' said Dad.

'You've got to help me, Lofty. It was an accident; I swear to God! Jesus—'

'Not in front of my girl,' said Dad, and Mr Mortlock glanced at Sadie as if seeing her for the first time. His face was haggard. Sadie shrank away from him.

Dad barked, 'Did anyone see you? Gerry, did anyone see you come here?'

Mr Mortlock licked his lips, then shook his head.

'You stay here,' said Dad. 'Don't move from this room. I'll lock the door. Sadie, you come with me.' He was a soldier again, rapping out orders. Dad was in charge; he'd make everything right.

Mr Mortlock lolled against the counter, his eyes closed. Dad motioned with his head, and Sadie followed him out of the shop, waiting while he turned the key. Dusk was falling.

'Evening, Clarry,' called Mrs Prescott across the street. 'Going to be a frost tonight, I should think.'

'Evening, Ethel.' Dad's voice was clear and calm. He put his arm around Sadie's shoulder and steered her along the road, past the pub, down the hill, past the Laycocks' house, across the railway tracks and past the Williams' place. He was walking fast, swinging his bad leg.

Once they were clear of the town, he led her off the road and into the bush. Leaves and twigs crunched beneath their shoes. The birds were shrieking their twilight chorus. The mallee gums twisted their grey arms into the sky.

Sadie helped Dad to cross the creek in the shallow place. They skirted round the graveyard where the first Mortlocks had buried their dead. Dad was leaning hard on her shoulder now.

'Do you want a rest, Dad?'

'No,' he said shortly. 'Almost there.'

She'd never seen the stones before. And yet, as they loomed out of the shadows, they chimed in her memory like something she already knew. They leaned from behind a tangle of trees, silent, watchful, solid clots of darkness in the shifting shadows.

Waaah!

A crow cried an abrupt warning, and a shudder ran through Sadie. For a fraction of a second, she knew that she was in the wrong time; she didn't belong here; she wanted to go home.

But then she heard a low groan, like no sound she'd ever heard, and all other thoughts fled.

'Dad! Over here!'

They knelt beside Jimmy.

'It's all right, mate, we're going to get help. You'll be all right,' said Dad.

'Nah,' whispered Jimmy. 'I'm done for.'

Sadie didn't know what to do. She reached out one shaking hand to Jimmy's head, and touched something wet and sticky, spongy, and a sharp edge of bone. She snatched her hand away.

Dad snapped, 'Keep back, Sadie!'

Jimmy murmured, 'You got your girl there? That Sadie there?'

Sadie swallowed. She whispered, 'I'm here, Jimmy.'

'I got something to tell your dad, Sadie.'

'What is it, Bird?'

There was a rustling in the darkness, as Jimmy fumbled in his pocket. Sadie heard him murmur, '...take care of this for me...not allowed to see...hide it, Clarry. Hide it good.'

The world had shrunk to a pinprick. All that existed was Jimmy's voice, his breath, the touch of his cold hand in the darkness.

'Bird?' whispered Dad. 'Come on, Bird...'

'You tell Netta...tell Netta...'

'I'll tell her, mate. Don't you worry, I'll tell her.'

An owl called, far away. The mournful notes fell like stones dropping into a deep pool, the ripples washing over the three of them, their hunched figures in the dark, small beneath the whispering trees.

Dad let out a breath. 'He's gone.'

A sob tore from Sadie's throat. She heard Dad shift in the darkness, rearranging his bad leg.

'Dad?' she whispered. 'We've got to fetch the police.' Her mind was racing. Mr Mortlock was locked into the shop. Mum and the little ones were shut up with a murderer. Somehow they'd have to get him inside the little lock-up cell behind the court-house, keep him there till they could fetch Constable McHugh. Mr Ransome from the pub could help, and George Tick from the draper's...

'No police!' Clarry's sergeant's bark rang out of the dark. Then he said, more gently, more like the Dad she knew, 'Hold on, love. I need to think.'

'Think about what?' Sadie heard her own shrill voice, the edge of panic. But there was no point panicking now; the worst had already happened. Jimmy was dead.

'Hold on, love. Shut up a minute.'

Sadie sat beside the body of the dead man. She realised she was rocking back and forth.

At last, Dad spoke. His voice was slow and heavy. 'Sadie, I've never asked you to do anything that's wrong, have I?'

'No, Dad. Of course not.'

'I'm sorry, love. I'm so sorry. But I'm going to ask you now.'

S adie stumbled through the bush, barely able to find her way between the trees in the moon-light. Her breath came in shallow gasps, as if she were drowning. The tears that had refused to fall when she sat beside Jimmy's body were spilling freely now; but they were tears of rage, of disbelief.

They couldn't tell the police, Dad had said. They had to help Mr Mortlock. They had to hide Jimmy's body and never tell anyone. 'I'll give him a Christian burial,' Dad said. 'I'll pray for his soul. He was a good man, Jimmy; he deserves that much.'

'What about his kids? What about Netta?' Sadie felt as if she were screaming; she was surprised to hear her voice barely louder than a whisper. 'You promised to tell her!'

'I'll tell her...' Dad hesitated. 'I'll tell her Jimmy's

had to go away. Or Gerald can tell her. We'll work something out between us.'

'Do you think she'll believe you?' said Sadie. 'Do you think if Mr Mortlock came and told Mum you'd *had to go away*, she'd believe it? That you'd go without saying goodbye? That you wouldn't come back? Don't you think his kids will miss him?'

'They go off walkabout all the time; it's normal to them,' said Dad. 'They're not like us, Sadie.'

Sadie's jaw clenched. Jimmy had bled to death like any man. Why would the colour of his skin make him different inside?

'Why are you doing this, Dad? *Why*?' And then Sadie's voice had risen to a scream, and Dad grabbed her arm and shook her.

'Be quiet, Sadie, for God's sake!'

'It's not right, Dad, you know it!'

'I have to help Gerald; I promised I'd look out for him.'

'And what about Jimmy? Didn't you promise him, too?' Her voice rose, shrill, hysterical. 'Jimmy was murdered! Gerald Mortlock should hang for this!'

Dad slapped her face.

'*Oh!*' Sadie sprang back, her hand to her cheek. Dad released her at once. They stood a few feet apart, breathing hard, beneath the moon.

'I owe Gerald Mortlock money,' said Dad. 'A lot of money.'

Sadie pressed her hand to her face. She said nothing.

'If anything happens to him, we're finished. Do you understand? I'll lose the shop, everything. You and your mum, the kids, we'll all be out on the street. Your mum doesn't know. What kind of job do you think I could find, with my lame leg and my busted lungs? I'm no use to anyone. If it wasn't for Gerald Mortlock, we'd be in the gutter, the lot of us. Is that what you want? *That's* why I'm doing this. For us, for the family. Now get along and do as I tell you.'

For a moment Sadie stood mute. Then she turned and began to stumble away, back through the bush toward the town. The stars peered down at her like hundreds of eyes in another world laid above this one.

Dad had forgotten to give her the key to the shop door, so she had to go in through the kitchen. The children were all around the table, finishing up their dinner. Rice pudding, Sadie noted distantly; she liked rice pudding. But she knew she'd eat nothing that night.

Four scared faces turned toward her as she entered. Mum rose from her chair.

'It's all right,' said Sadie quickly. 'Don't worry. Dad'll be back later.'

Mum followed her into the passage. 'Sadie, what's happened?'

'I can't tell you, Mum. There's things Dad wants me to do.' Seeing Mum's pale face, Sadie felt as if she were the adult and Mum the child. She touched Mum's arm. 'Keep the kids out of the way.'

Dad had said, *Stay with him, Sadie. Fetch a cloth and let him wash. Give him my other shirt; he can't be seen in those clothes. And keep the door locked.*

From her parents' bedroom, she snatched Dad's Sunday shirt and the old patched trousers he wore for working in the vegetable patch, a flannel cloth and the basin from the washstand in the corner. She could hear the kids' subdued chatter from the kitchen, and her mother's low, strained voice trying to hush them. Sadie hurried into the shop and closed the door carefully behind her.

Mr Mortlock had lit a lamp. But he was slumped on the floor against the counter again. A brand new tin of Blue Crane cigarettes sat open beside him, and he was smoking. The shop was cloudy with smoke.

He turned his head when he heard the door. 'Where's Clarry?'

Sadie couldn't answer. She couldn't even look at him.

'Was he … Did I …?'

'He's dead,' said Sadie.

Mr Mortlock took a long drag on his cigarette. He closed his eyes and said again, 'Where's Clarry?'

'He—' Sadie swallowed. 'He's going to bury—'
She choked on Jimmy's name; she couldn't speak it.
'—the body.'

Mr Mortlock's shoulders sagged. 'Thank God,
thank God,' he muttered. 'I knew I could count on
Clarry.' He dashed tears from his eyes and wiped his
nose on his sleeve.

Sadie felt a wave of revulsion. 'Here.' She indi-
cated the flannel and the basin. 'You can wash.'

He looked up at her, then held out his hands for
her to wash them.

Sadie stared. She wasn't his mother, or his servant.
But Dad had said they had to help him. She made
herself kneel beside him.

She shook with wordless anger, with disgust, as
she wrung out the cloth and sponged Mr Mortlock's
hands, his murdering hands, smeared with dried
blood. How had he done it? With a rock? With a
tree branch? Did he shoot him? The jagged hole in
the back of Jimmy's head... Sadie felt sick.

She wouldn't think about that. She'd remember
Jimmy as he was. Big kind Jimmy with his broad
smile, firm and muscular as a horse, his eyes that
seemed to see right through you.

Thinking of Jimmy alive was even worse than
thinking of him dead. *He was worth ten of you*, she
wanted to shout. But she said nothing.

She rinsed out the flannel and a brown stain swirled through the water. She stood up and stepped away from him.

'Dad says you're to change your clothes.' She held out the shirt and the old trousers. 'I'll be back in a minute.'

She let herself out into the passage and pressed her forehead against the cold wood of the door. She'd count to a hundred; that would give him enough time. She wished Dad would come back; she wished Mum would bustle out of the kitchen and take over.

But no one came to save her. She was alone.

She wondered how Dad would manage. He'd have to limp to the Mortlock outbuildings and look for a shovel in one of the sheds. At least Jimmy would be buried in the bush with the birds around him and those big old stones to watch over him. That was as good as any church.

She counted to a hundred and twenty, and let herself into the shop.

Mr Mortlock had changed his clothes. His bloodied shirt and trousers were rolled into a bundle on the floor, and he was lighting up another cigarette. He looked at Sadie as he shook out the match, and sucked in a lungful of smoke.

'That's better,' he said. 'Steadies the nerves. Got any brandy?'

Sadie shook her head. She stayed behind the counter, glad to have its bulk between herself and him.

He blew out a cloud of smoke and stared up at the ceiling. 'It was an accident, you know.'

Sadie said nothing.

'He came rushing up to me. Would have thought he'd had a few, he was that wild, only Jimmy never drinks. Even in France, he never had a drink. Not even a beer.' Mr Mortlock closed his eyes. Sadie had the feeling that he'd been transported somewhere far away, to a different world. Then his eyes flicked open and he was back, his stare blazing so intently into her face that she was frightened.

'He was wild. Shouting and bunching his fists up, getting ready to take a swing at me. Thought he must have been bitten by a mad dog.' Mr Mortlock bared his teeth in a mirthless grin. 'Shouting something about the new dam. Couldn't understand what he was on about. He was dead against it right from the start; don't know why. Got some funny notion in his head, the way they do. I said, "Settle down, Jimmy. Keep your hair on." Well, he didn't like that much. Came right up to me, breathing in my face.' Mr Mortlock stared at Sadie. 'No respect. Couldn't let him get away with that.'

Sadie stared at the floor. *I wish I could take a cloth*

to those shelves, she thought. *He's left marks everywhere.* She was seized with a desire to scrub the whole shop from top to bottom, to sweep away all trace of Mr Mortlock, to cleanse the place of his taint, his sin, his awful crime...

'Had to defend myself, didn't I,' said Mr Mortlock abruptly. 'Anyone could see that. He was like a bloody madman.' He paced up and down the shop, flicking ash on the floor. 'The gun went off while we were struggling. That's what happened. It was an accident.'

He glanced sharply at Sadie. 'That's what happened,' he repeated.

Sadie heard herself say, 'Either it was an accident, or you were defending yourself. It can't be both.'

Mr Mortlock's face hardened. 'I said it was an accident, didn't I? You better watch your tongue, Miss Hazzard.'

Sadie dropped her eyes. *If it wasn't for Gerald Mortlock, we'd all be in the gutter.*

She groped for Dad's stool to steady herself. The smell of the smoke was making her feel sick; if she had to listen to Mr Mortlock say another word, she'd scream. She'd scream and scream until they heard her in Bendigo, until the police came running, until they took him away...

But that wouldn't bring Jimmy Raven back.

Oh, please, Dad, hurry, don't leave me here with him. I can't bear it.

But it seemed like hours they waited, trapped there together. Sadie heard the usual commotion of the little ones getting ready for bed, feet thumping along the floorboards; she even heard the low hum of voices behind the wall as they said their prayers. Sadie stared at the back of Mr Mortlock's head. *What would he say in his prayers tonight?*

And then she remembered that she hadn't prayed for Jimmy's soul. She bowed her head, but the right words wouldn't come. *Our Father,* she began, *give us this day our daily trespasses, for thy kingdom will be done...*

She remembered that she'd had no dinner. She was hollow inside.

Mr Mortlock smoked one cigarette after another. He didn't offer to pay. For the sake of tidiness, Sadie picked up the empty tin off the counter and stuffed it into her cardigan pocket.

It was after midnight when they heard Dad's key in the lock.

Mr Mortlock jumped up, and ground out the last cigarette under his heel. The shop bell tinkled, and Sadie's head seemed full of its jangling, bursting with the noise of bells, as if her skull would split. Dad limped in, his face grey, his clothes stained with mud and blood.

'Well?' demanded Mr Mortlock.

'It's done.' Dad bolted the door and leaned against the wall as if his bones had turned to jelly. His face was like wax. 'He's in the old graveyard. It seemed the least we could do for him.'

No! Sadie wanted to cry. *Not there!* She felt like weeping. She knew Dad meant it as a sign of respect, the only sign he felt he could give, but it seemed all wrong. Jimmy should have been buried near the stones, under the trees, in the heart of the bush. He wouldn't have wanted to lie with the Mortlocks...

Somewhere out in the ice-cold night, a crow shrieked. The sound pierced her like a knife of freezing iron.

'Sadie?' Dad glanced at her. 'You all right, love?'

She tried to reply, but her tongue was numb in her mouth. She sank to the floor, her head spinning, and the shop went black around her.

'You all right, love?'

Sadie opened her eyes. Mrs Fox had emerged from behind the checkout and was bending over her, her face wrinkled with concern.

'You had a funny turn, love?'

Sadie managed to sit up. 'Yeah – something like that.' She tried to stand, and collapsed back to the floor.

'Stay there, love, keep your head down. You want some water?'

Sadie shook her head. 'Could you . . .' She hated how feeble her voice sounded, hardly more than a whisper. 'Could you please ring my mum to come and get me?'

'Don't be silly, love, I'll run you home myself. *Brayden!*' she snapped, and Fox shuffled forward, chewing his rat's tail. 'Go and get my handbag out the locker at the back. We're taking poor little Sadie home.'

Sadie dragged herself upright and drew her knees under her chin. She wished Mrs Fox wouldn't stare at her.

'You're not in trouble, are you, love?' Fox's mum asked suddenly. 'You know, pregnant?'

'*No!*'

'No harm in asking,' said Mrs Fox, injured.

If she could just count to a hundred, she'd be okay, thought Sadie. Everything would be okay.

She squeezed her eyes shut and began to count.

Ellie sat on the edge of the bed and patted Sadie's knee through the covers. 'I want you to come into the hospital with me and have some tests. We need to sort this out.'

Sadie curled herself into a tight, defensive ball, arms wrapped around her knees. She mumbled, 'Just because I felt woozy for a minute, it doesn't mean there's something wrong with me.'

'People don't faint for no reason.'

'I feel fine now.'

'But not fine enough to go to school?'

'Well, one day off couldn't *hurt*,' said Sadie hopefully.

'Hm.' Ellie stroked back her hair. 'Let me know if you feel woozy again, okay?'

Sadie wriggled down in the bed, but Ellie didn't leave. She picked at the edge of the sheet.

'Sadie?' Ellie said at last. 'If you do hate it here – I mean, *really* hate it – we can always go back to the city.'

Sadie stared. 'But you sold our house.'

Ellie laughed. 'There are other houses. Melbourne's a big place. And I could find another job.'

Sadie said slowly, 'What about David?'

Ellie looked away. 'It's early days with me and David...and you come first. You know that, don't you?'

There was a pause.

'I don't hate it here,' said Sadie. 'I kind of like it now.'

'Really?' The depth of relief in her mother's voice told Sadie how much it would cost Ellie to leave Boort.

She said more firmly, 'Yeah. You were right, the country is beautiful. The lake's really pretty. It's nice having all the frogs and sheep and birds around. And our family comes from here. We belong here, don't we?'

Ellie smiled. 'I guess we do.' She stood up. 'But still, I shouldn't have rushed into moving us here. I should have talked to you about it first.' She took a deep breath. 'I'm sorry.'

Sadie was so surprised she could hardly speak. Ellie had never apologised to her before, about anything. She said in a rush, 'I'm sorry, too – about being grumpy, and not helping, and stuff.'

Ellie kissed her forehead. Then she went out, gently closing the door behind her.

Sadie stared up at the flickering of shadows and morning light on her ceiling. Now she'd seen Clarry and Jean, now she'd inhabited the other Sadie's skin, she felt tied to Boort by long ropes of history, threading back through Mum and Grandpa Phil...

The memory of the previous night gripped her with the sudden chill of a nightmare. The sticky horror of Jimmy's smashed skull beneath her fingertips; the long bulk of his body under the trees. The blood. Gerald Mortlock's twisted face, the wreathing clouds of cigarette smoke. *I killed the bugger. Jimmy Raven's dead.*

What if she, as the other Sadie, had defied her father's orders and told the police what she'd seen that night? Would that have changed everything? If Gerald Mortlock was arrested for murder, would she have returned to a present without Mortlocks, without Invergarry, where the dam had never been built, Cross Creek still flowed, and the dried-up lake had never existed?

No Mortlocks would mean no Lachie.

If the Hazzards had lost their shop, if they'd become homeless, maybe baby Philip would have become sick and died. Then there would be no Ellie, and there'd be no Sadie.

And besides – a chill struck her heart – if Sadie had reported Gerald Mortlock, Clarry would have been arrested too. He'd hidden Jimmy's body; he'd covered up the crime. That made him a – what was it called? – a helper to murder. An *accessory*, that was it. The other Sadie believed Mr Mortlock ought to be hanged. What if they'd hanged Clarry, too?

She had to find out what had happened to Gerald Mortlock. The Crow said, *when the Law is broken, there must be punishment.* Maybe the story wasn't over; maybe punishment had come to Mr Mortlock after all.

Clinging to that thought like a lifeline, she fell asleep.

The next day was Saturday. After breakfast, Ellie stopped Sadie on her way out the door. 'Where are you going?'

'For a walk.'

'You sure you're well enough? Don't go yet. Wait and take Walter with you, he and David will be here soon.' Ellie looked sly. 'We've got a surprise for you.'

'What kind of surprise?' said Sadie warily.

'It comes in tins.'

Sadie spread her hands, mystified.

'We're going to paint your room! David's bringing the paint.'

Sadie threw her arms around Ellie.

'See?' laughed Ellie, breathless. 'I do think about you sometimes. I'm not the world's *worst* mother.'

'Second or third worst, at least,' Sadie assured her.

After that, she didn't feel she could say no to taking Walter, even though she'd planned to go on her own.

Ellie and David chatted as they spread out old sheets in Sadie's room, apparently unaware that Sadie and Walter could hear every word they said.

'... seem to be getting on well, don't they?'

'... good for each other. They both need a friend...'

Walter and Sadie caught each other's eye, embarrassed. Sadie grimaced; then Walter smiled his rare smile.

'I don't have to come,' he said. 'If you'd rather be on your own.'

'If you stay, they'll make you paint,' said Sadie. 'You can come.'

And she found, once they'd begun walking, that she was quite glad to have him with her. Walter was quiet; he let her think her own thoughts. And his solid presence beside her was unexpectedly reassuring.

He only said, 'Where are we going?' and when Sadie told him, 'The cemetery,' he just nodded.

It was a long walk. The Boort town cemetery was a few kilometres north-west of town, surrounded by flat, empty farmland. Sheep stared as they passed, and the wind moaned softly in the low trees that fringed the graveyard.

Sadie walked along the neat, broad paths, searching for the older graves, peering at each inscription, walking back in time: 1976, 1968, 1951, 1943. The further back she went, the wilder the weeds and thistles grew, obscuring the stone crosses and crooked headstones.

'You looking for someone?' said Walter.

Sadie hesitated. 'Looking for ghosts.'

'Shouldn't do that.' Walter's voice was serious. 'Don't want ghosts to come looking for you.'

Sadie slashed at the long grass with a stick, her heart in her throat as she glanced at each grave. *James Wilfred Gott, aged 65 years. Mary Horatia Tick, aged 4 months, At Rest In Jesus. Percy Williams, Loved Husband and Father, He Served,* with the rising sun badge of a soldier.

And then she saw it.

It was a low, plain grave, a long box of unadorned grey granite.

Gerald Stanley Mortlock
26ᵗʰ March 1896 – 3ʳᵈ August 1933.

August 1933. He died that same year. He had been
punished after all.

Sadie's eyes flew to the next headstone.

HAZZARD, Clarence John
4ᵗʰ June 1894 – 12ᵗʰ September 1933
Beloved Husband of Jean,
Devoted Father of Sarah, John, Mabel (dec),
Elizabeth and Philip.
Sorely Missed.

Sadie felt breathless. Clarry had died only a month
after Gerald Mortlock. That was a strange coinci-
dence. And he'd left poor Jean with all those children
to look after, little Betty and baby Philip – they
wouldn't even remember their father… And there
was the extra baby, Mabel, between John and Betty.
She hadn't known about Mabel…

She was still thinking about the poor little baby as
her eyes scanned the bottom of the gravestone. There
was a second inscription, obscured with lichen. Sadie
scratched at the letters with her stick, and then all at
once the words leapt out at her.

Also His Daughter
Sarah Louise (Sadie)
1920–1934
Aged 14 Years.
Tragically Taken.

'You all right?' said Walter behind her.

Sadie put out a hand blindly and clutched at his arm.

'She died!' Sadie heard the note of hysteria in her voice as her fingers tightened round Walter's arm. 'She died, too!'

'You want to sit down?' said Walter. 'You don't look too good.'

Sadie allowed herself to be led to the dappled shade of a ragged gum tree, and collapsed onto a wooden bench.

'That girl had the same name as you,' said Walter. 'Must be pretty weird, seeing that. Nearly your age, too.'

Mutely Sadie nodded. They'd all died. Within a year, all three of them were dead – Gerald, Clarry, even Sadie. She wondered what had happened to them.

When the Law is broken there must be punishment.

Walter said, 'With my people, with traditional people, when someone dies, you don't say their name no more. From respect, but also, you know, in case their spirit comes back to get you.'

Sadie said, 'You believe in ghosts?'

'Sure I do,' said Walter. 'You?'

'Yes,' said Sadie. 'I do.'

They sat side by side in silence.

'I saw my dad after he died,' said Walter at last. He scratched at his shoe with the stem of a gum leaf. 'I dreamed I'd come and live with David, and I did. Dreamed the house, too. And I dreamed about you before I met you. Didn't see your face, but I know it was you, now.' Walter flicked the leaf aside. 'In that dream, you told me you could talk to crows.' He turned to stare at her. 'Can you?'

'Yes,' said Sadie.

Walter looked away again. 'David doesn't believe this stuff. The old ways are all gone, he says. We got to live in the world like it is now. I don't tell him about my dreams. But I tell Auntie Lily. I told her my dream about you, about the crow-girl. She said I'd meet you one day. She said you'd have a story to tell me.'

'Yes,' said Sadie. 'I do.'

Walter didn't look at her while she spoke. He tipped his head back and gazed up at the sky, veiled by the branches of the gum tree.

She told him everything. About the crows – or perhaps it was always the same crow – who spoke to her. About the circle of stones. About Clarry and Jimmy and Gerald and that last terrible night. When she told him how she'd become the other Sadie, she faltered; but he didn't laugh or scoff. He just said, 'Yep,' and waited for her to go on.

'And now, today,' she said at last. 'Seeing those gravestones, Gerald and Clarry and Sadie, all dying so close together, so soon after…' Her voice faded away.

A flock of pink-and-grey galahs chattered overhead, trailing their noise like a banner across the sky.

'It's – spooky,' she finished lamely. She wished she had a better word than *spooky* for the sense of dread that crept across her skin and crawled in the pit of her stomach.

Walter spat out a leaf stem and stood up, a dark silhouette against the bright horizon. Sadie shaded her eyes.

He said, 'Better go and look at that lake, I reckon. See if we can find where Jimmy Raven's buried.'

Of course. That was what she ought to do. Sadie felt her face crack with relief; it wasn't exactly a smile.

'Come on,' she said. 'I'll show you.'

T hey heard the whine of the trail bikes from the edge of the lake, a distant drone like giant wasps. Sadie stopped.

'Someone's out there.'

'Might be a long way away,' said Walter. 'Hard to tell, noise echoing round like that.'

Sadie nodded and slowly walked out onto the crust of yellow mud. But with every step, her stomach churned. The roar of the bikes grew louder as she and Walter crossed the lake.

'I think the graves are over there—' she began, but then she saw the bikes. Dark shapes were zooming up and around the cup of the secret valley, the place where the circle of stones lay hidden. A big battered four-wheel drive and a mud-spattered ute were parked nearby.

Sadie felt sick. 'They shouldn't be there!' She broke into a run, and Walter ran beside her.

Music blared from the site, a thudding bass that made the ground tremble. Sadie pulled up, panting for breath; anger glowed in her like fire.

Craig Mortlock was lounging against one of the stones, a ring of empty beer cans littered around his legs like a tawdry copy of the stone circle itself. Lachie was perched on another rock, swinging his legs, his bike parked nearby. Sadie recognised two older men, mates of Craig's, from the front bar of the pub. One of the riders on the swooping bikes was Hammer, the boy with no neck. The other had stiff, straw-coloured hair and furious acne; Sadie had never seen him before.

Sadie and Walter stood at the very edge of the stone circle. Craig Mortlock crumpled a beer can and dropped it at his feet. 'G'day, kids.'

'Hello,' said Sadie. Her mouth was as dry as the lake bed.

'Hi.' Lachie rubbed his nose and avoided Sadie's eyes.

'And what can we do for you?' said Craig.

One of the bikes wove between two stones, spun its back wheel in the mud and roared off again. Red rage burned inside Sadie.

'You shouldn't do that,' she said.

Craig cupped his hand to his ear. 'Can't hear you, love. If you've got something to say, you'll have to speak up.'

'You shouldn't do that!' shouted Sadie, clenching her fists. 'This is a special place! It's not for *picnics*, it's not a *bike trail*.'

Craig's eyebrows shot into his hair. 'Excuse me, darling. Didn't realise you were an expert. Been taking lessons from your boyfriend?' He jerked his chin at Walter.

Somebody guffawed. Sadie thrust her head high. 'This is a special place. You know it is.'

'I beg to differ,' said Craig. 'Even your mum's boyfriend says it's not worth any money, and I bet he knows more about it than you do.' He pointed his finger at Sadie. 'Believe me, love, if it was worth anything, I'd be the first one to rope it off and flog it to the Council of Aboriginal Welfare or whoever. But nobody wants it.' He straightened up. 'You should be pleased! Look at all these people, experiencing a bit of Aboriginal culture!' He waved his arm at the men sprawled against the rocks, their boots resting on the carvings, their cans tossed into the centre of the circle. 'At least people are getting to see it, eh?'

As if on cue, the bikes drew up to the stone circle, sputtered, and stopped. A sudden silence fell. Everyone was staring at Sadie and Walter.

'You got no respect,' said Walter very quietly.

But Craig heard him. 'You think you can march onto my land, the land my family's owned and farmed and looked after for five generations, and lecture me about respect? You've got a bloody cheek, son!'

Sadie said, 'This land belonged to his people, way before your family got here!'

'No, it didn't,' said Lachie. He crushed a Coke can in his hand. 'He doesn't even come from round here. He comes from up on the border, from the river, same as his uncle David. They don't belong here. Us Mortlocks have been living here longer than his family have.'

'Too right,' said Craig.

Lachie glanced at his father, and flushed slightly. 'I was born here,' he said to Walter. 'And I've lived here all my life, and so has my dad, and his dad, and his dad before him. Who do you reckon this land belongs to? Not to you, mate. There's none of your people left round here. They're *gone*.'

'That's not true!' cried Sadie. 'David and Walter have family in Boort, there are heaps of Aboriginal people around here!'

But Walter shook his head. He said softly, 'All our people got mixed up in the reserves. Weren't allowed to speak our languages, weren't allowed to keep up the old ways. Nobody really knows who comes from where. It's all mixed up. Lots of things forgotten. Auntie Lily says this is Dja Dja Wurrung land. But they weren't allowed to stay here. They had to move south, had to leave their country. This is a Dja Dja Wurrung place.'

Craig rose to his feet, scowling. 'I've heard enough from you two. You're trespassing. Now get off my land.'

'People died here!' screamed Sadie. 'Don't you care? Your grandfather killed a man. Even if you won't show respect to the crows, can't you show respect for *him*?'

'What's this bull about my grandfather?' said Craig. 'He never killed anyone!'

'He did; he murdered Jimmy Raven!'

Lachie screwed his face up. 'What's she crapping on about?'

'Buggered if I know. Now *get out*!' bellowed Craig.

'He was a murderer!' Sadie shrieked. 'The Crow knows. This is Crow's land, Crow's country; he knows what happened; he punished them! And he'll punish you, too!'

'Kid's flipped out,' said one of the men. 'Gone mental.'

Lachie slid from his rock. 'You heard what Dad said. Now piss off!'

Sadie heard Walter hiss between his teeth like a warning; she saw Lachie wave his fists; she heard Hammer shout, 'Get him, Lachie!' and she saw Craig's face, red and bullish. Then all at once, Lachie and Walter were struggling together, wrestling, pushing at each other.

'Walter!' she shouted in sudden fear. Walter mustn't fight; he mustn't get into trouble again. 'Come on, let's go!'

But he didn't hear her. He was smaller than Lachie, but he was nimble and wiry, and Lachie couldn't seem to get a grip on him. *Oh, crows!* Sadie sent out a desperate, silent cry. *Help us!*

One of the men swore, and scrambled up. 'Look at that! Up there—'

All the men stared at the sky, frozen in disbelief. Walter and Lachie broke apart, panting, and lifted their faces. Sadie's mouth dropped open.

Hundreds of black crows came silently wheeling through the sky toward them. Without a sound, they eddied high above the dried lake, a thickening, churning mass of birds, a black whirlpool in the sky.

'Lord Almighty,' whispered Craig Mortlock. 'What the hell?'

The cloud of crows seemed to tighten around the circle of stones. One by one, the men stepped backward until they had cleared the space. Lachie ran for his bike and clutched it like a shield. Mute, sinister, with the rustle of a thousand wings, the crows wheeled lower and lower, tighter and tighter. Sadie saw the gleam of hundreds of beaks, jet black and glistening.

Walter touched Sadie's shoulder. Their eyes met, and they ran. Sadie found Walter's hand groping for hers. She grabbed it and gripped hard. Slipping and sliding, they pelted across the yellow mud. The cloud of crows blotted out the sun; a shadow spread like ink across the valley.

It wasn't until they reached the edge of the lake bed, the edge of the shadow, and were safe again in the winter sunlight, that they dared to stop and look back.

A gunshot cracked across the valley.

The cloud of birds exploded, scattering like black sparks from a firework. The air filled with caws of alarm, the panicked beating of innumerable wings. Instinctively, Sadie ducked. Another gunshot echoed across the lake, and another.

'They're shooting the crows!' screamed Sadie.

Wah! Wah! Wah! Crows flapped away in all directions. Wings whirred above Sadie and Walter's heads. And still the shots rang out.

'We have to stop them!' cried Sadie.

But she knew, as Walter did, that there was nothing they could do. They could only stand helplessly and watch as the crows scattered, and count them as some fell, like black stones, from the empty sky.

'It's all my fault,' said Sadie. 'I called them, and they came.'

'Not your fault,' said Walter. 'You didn't know the men were going to start shooting.'

'I didn't know they were going to come,' said Sadie. There was a short silence while they trudged along the road. Then Sadie repeated dully, 'It's all my fault.'

'Not your fault,' said Walter again. He halted in front of the supermarket. 'You wait there. Better not come in. Don't want you having any more flashbacks.'

He came out with two bottles of lemonade. 'Auntie Vonn says something sweet's the best thing when you've had a shock.'

The lemonade was delicious. Sadie suddenly

realised how hungry she was. She hoped Ellie had made a huge lunch.

'Car's gone,' observed Walter as they neared the house. 'David and Ellie must've gone to the footy already. We're playing Charlton today.'

'But then why were Craig and Lachie hanging round at the dry lake? They should be at the footy too.'

Walter shrugged. 'Plenty of time till kick-off.' He glanced at the sun. 'Another hour, maybe? David's got to get there early for coaching, but Craig and Lachie don't. We're playing at home; it's not far to the oval.'

Sadie liked the way he called Boort *we*. 'They'll wonder where we are. David and Mum, I mean.'

'They won't care,' said Walter. 'Long as we're getting on okay, we could go to the moon and they wouldn't care.' He shot Sadie one of his swift, rare grins.

The house was locked. Sadie fished for the key that Ellie hid in the gumboot by the back door. 'I guess we can make cheese on toast,' she was beginning to say, when she heard Walter's sharp intake of breath, and turned around.

A crow was in the garden.

It was slightly larger than an ordinary crow. It opened its beak, but no sound came out. It lifted one stiff wing, and Sadie saw a sticky patch that marred the smooth gloss of its feathers. Blood.

Sadie pressed her hand to her mouth. 'I'm so sorry,' she whispered.

The crow's round eye regarded her coldly. 'The Law is broken.'

'I know I shouldn't have taken Lachie there,' said Sadie wretchedly. 'It's all my fault—'

But the crow spoke over her. 'What was lost must be found. What was stolen must be returned.'

'What are you talking about *now*?' cried Sadie in despair. 'Why can't you just *tell* me?'

The crow's head swivelled. He stared at Walter.

'The story goes on, as it always goes on. The Law is broken and there is punishment. The dead cannot live again, but what was taken from the clever man must be returned. When the Law is broken the world is broken. The circle must be joined again.'

Sadie snatched a glance at Walter. He was looking down, his eyes wide, shaking his head slowly from side to side.

'Do you want us to find something?' asked Sadie desperately. 'You have to tell us what it is! What was taken?'

The crow spread his wings and cried out in pain. *Waaah!*

'*Please* tell us!' cried Sadie. 'How can we know what to do if you won't tell us?'

The crow rolled his eye in her direction. He didn't call her a fool, but he was clearly thinking it.

'You cannot know all of Crow's stories,' he said. 'And Crow cannot know all of yours. Your story is dark to Crow, as Crow's stories are hidden from you. You must find the place where the stories cross, and there you will find what is lost. Join the circle, mend what is broken.'

'But how—'

The crow gave a last anguished croak of *waa-waaah!* 'The crows will help you. When you call, the crows will come.'

And then he was gone.

Sadie spun around to Walter. 'Did you hear it? Did you hear it speak?'

Walter rubbed his eyes. 'Yeah, I heard him.' He sounded dazed.

'Its wing was hurt; did you see?' said Sadie. 'They must have shot it.'

Walter stared at her. 'His *wing*? But he was a man.'

Sadie stared back. 'It was a crow!'

'A man and a crow at the same time,' said Walter. 'A messenger from Waa, the Crow. A spirit shaped like a man. A man with a bleeding arm.' He shivered and sat down abruptly on a garden chair.

Sadie sat down heavily in the other chair. 'Why won't they just tell us what they want us to do, instead of talking in riddles? Unless – did *you* understand?'

Walter shrugged. 'He was talking about the Law, and stories, and something lost. Didn't make any sense to me.'

'Something stolen from the clever man,' said Sadie.

'A clever man means someone with special powers,' said Walter. 'Someone who knows about magic and spirits. Like Auntie Lily.'

'Oh!' said Sadie. She remembered the figure of the crow in Walter's painting. 'Did *she* lose something?'

'I dunno. I don't think so.'

They sat silently in the afternoon sun. Leaves rustled and danced in the breeze. Sadie shivered, and hugged herself. 'Let's go inside. I'm starving.'

Walter didn't move. He said slowly, 'She could help us.'

'Auntie Lily?'

'No, the tooth fairy. Of course, Auntie Lily.'

'You think she'll believe us?'

'I've told her about my dreams and that. She was good. She knows about this stuff.'

Sadie shook her head. 'No way. We can't tell anyone. I shouldn't have told Lachie. I probably shouldn't even have told you. Except…' She hesitated. 'You did hear it talking, too, so I guess that was all right… But we can't go round telling people we've been going back in time and hearing crows talk. They'll think we're psycho. Mum would freak out.'

'Not saying we should tell *people*. Not your mum, not David. Just Auntie Lily.'

'No. We can't. It's secret.'

Walter stared up at the sky. 'I can tell her what I saw today. That's my story, too. That's not our secret. You can't stop me talking about that.'

'But she'll think we're crazy!'

Walter said nothing.

'Right,' said Sadie. 'Fine. Whatever.'

She stomped inside, banging the door behind her. She dragged out bread and cheese; she was so hungry she couldn't wait to assemble it into a sandwich, but tore a hunk off the loaf and stuffed it into her mouth. She could see Walter through the window, hunched on the garden chair, hands clasped between his knees, unmoving.

'I don't *want* to!' she said aloud, as if they were still arguing. 'I don't want to tell anyone else.'

But she knew, even as she spoke, that they needed help. The crows had chosen her, but she couldn't understand what they were talking about; she didn't know what they wanted from her.

You cannot know all Crow's stories, and Crow cannot know yours.

The crows had shown her the story that belonged to her, to her family – the story of Clarry and Gerald and Jimmy Raven, the other Sadie's story. *Find the place where the stories cross*, the crow said. But what did that mean?

It seemed that she and the crows were supposed to help each other, but how? Would Auntie Lily know?

Walter stayed stubbornly hunched outside.

Sadie slapped some cheese between two wedges of bread, slid it onto a plate, and wandered out of the kitchen. The whole house smelled faintly of paint fumes. Her bedroom! She'd forgotten that Mum and David had been painting her room.

Her furniture was jumbled in the hall. She took her sandwich into the bedroom. It was transformed: the hated flowery wallpaper had disappeared beneath a lilac-tinged wash of paint. The room seemed bigger, lighter.

She touched one wall gently with her fingertip. Up close, the raised pattern of the wallpaper was still just discernable. And what lay under the wallpaper, how many layers of paint and colour? And after she was gone, some stranger might paint over her lilac, bury it under cream or green or yellow or stripes... How many layers would line these walls before the house crumbled?

Layer upon layer, story upon story…

In 1933, Gerald Mortlock killed Jimmy Raven, and Clarry Hazzard hid it, and Gerald and Clarry died. Three friends, all dead, and Sadie dead, too. *Punished.* That story was covered up, buried, but that didn't mean that it wasn't still there. Blame and bitterness, trickling through the years like poison, bleeding through like the pattern of the wallpaper. All the stories, all the joys and tragedies laid on top of each other like transparencies, each one smudging and blurring the rest until it was impossible to tell what the truth was. Stories building up a residue on the land, like layers of dried yellow silt, with the bones of the past thrusting through…

Sadie realised with a start that Walter had moved silently into the room behind her, a box of cheesy biscuits in his hand.

'I am going to tell Auntie,' he said.

Sadie traced an invisible swirl on the wall with her finger. 'Okay,' she said, after a moment. 'But I want to come too. And just Auntie – not Mum or David.'

Walter nodded. 'Going round there tomorrow,' he said. 'To Auntie Lily and Auntie Vonn's. You can come.'

'Okay,' said Sadie. She felt a weight lift from her stomach and knew it was right.

'Room looks good,' said Walter.

'Yeah, it does.'

He dug out a handful of biscuits, and pointed toward the living room with his chin. 'There's footy on the TV. Bulldogs versus Freo.'

Sadie followed him and plumped down on the couch. On the television, the crowd on the far side of the desert gave a tinny roar as the ball flew between the goalposts.

'Good game?' said Sadie.

'Nah. They're killing them.'

Walter passed her the box, and they sat side by side, companionably munching, until there was nothing left but crumbs.

W alter told David that he and Sadie were
doing an oral history project for school.

'I thought you were in different years?'
said Ellie.

'Getting kids in different levels to work together,'
said Walter, without missing a beat.

'That's right,' Sadie chipped in. 'Building bonds
across the school community.'

'Sounds good,' said David. 'All right, why not?'
He tossed his car keys in the air and looked at Ellie.
'If the kids are at Vonn's place all afternoon, we could
drive down to Bendigo and grab some lunch maybe?'

'Lunch with the game-winning hero coach of the
Boort Football Club? How can I refuse? You should
have been there,' she said to Sadie. 'We *smashed*
Charlton. It was beautiful to watch.'

'Yeah, you said.' Sadie rolled her eyes at Walter. 'About a million times.'

David dropped them at Auntie Lily's house, a tiny, shabby weatherboard cottage at the edge of town. As the car drew up, a crowd of children spilled out of the house, shouting for David's attention.

'This is my friend, Ellie, and her daughter, Sadie,' called David over the racket.

'You coming in for a cuppa?' A large, deep-voiced woman in swathes of red and orange stood on the porch with her arms folded across her ample chest, staring hard at Ellie.

David looked at Ellie. 'Ah...Don't know if we've got time, Vonn...'

Ellie smiled. 'We'll bring everyone back a treat from Bendigo, okay?' She waved her arm across the crowd of children. There was an instant clamour of approval.

Vonn nodded slowly and uncrossed her arms.

David said, 'Walter and Sadie want to talk to Auntie. That all right?'

'She might be asleep,' warned Vonn. 'But they can go in.' She stood back to let Walter and Sadie slip inside.

The kitchen was full of women drinking tea, smoking, laughing. They greeted Walter with cries of delight; they all wanted to hug and kiss him, passing him around the table from one set of arms to the next. Sadie shrank shyly into a corner.

'I'll take you in,' said Vonn. She dropped a hand on Sadie's shoulder and propelled her down the hallway. Walter extricated himself and followed. Vonn knocked softly at a door and waited until a voice called, 'Come in.'

The bedroom was dim, the curtains drawn. Sadie could just make out a figure propped on pillows in the bed.

'Auntie Lily? Walter's here.'

'Eh, beautiful boy!' Auntie Lily was an old, old lady with wispy white hair. She reached out two hands to draw Walter to her for a kiss. 'You never come to see your auntie no more?'

'I'm sorry,' said Walter humbly.

Sadie hung back during the greeting and scolding. Then Vonn beckoned her closer. 'Auntie, Walter brought a friend to meet you.'

'Eh?' Auntie Lily squinted at her.

'We want to ask you something,' said Walter.

Auntie Lily patted the edge of the bed. 'Sit down, sit down. I got time for a chat today, I reckon.'

Vonn withdrew. 'Don't tire her out,' she warned, before she shut the door.

Outside, Sadie could hear shrieks and yells beating around the tiny house like a whirlwind. It reached a crescendo of cheers, then faded into the distance. Sadie could imagine the wave of kids running down the road after David and Ellie's departing car. Her mum would love all that attention, thought Sadie rather wistfully; she enjoyed crowds of kids. She always said she wished she'd had more children.

Walter perched on the edge of the bed and began to talk earnestly to Auntie Lily. The old woman leaned forward intently, peering into his face. Sadie saw that her eyes were milky, that she must be almost blind. Sadie wasn't sure that Auntie Lily even knew she was in the room. She was too shy to sit on the bed.

Walter sat close to the old woman. His voice rose and fell like the murmur of a creek. The stone circle, the crows. Sadie shifted impatiently in her corner. He wasn't telling it properly; he hadn't started at the beginning; he was leaving things out. She couldn't hear what he was saying. Auntie Lily nodded, murmured in reply. At one point she began to tell Walter a rambling legend, about how Crow had stolen something from the moon. Sadie's foot twitched. What did that have to do with anything?

At last Walter told Auntie Lily what Crow's messenger had said to them in Sadie's backyard, about returning what was stolen from the clever man. Auntie Lily's expression suddenly seemed to sharpen; her gnarled old hand shot out and gripped Walter's tight.

'My uncle, he was a clever man,' she said. 'He was killed, you know, long time ago. Got in a fight, some bugger shot him. Never find his body. My auntie, she look all over; never find him. They tell her he gone away. But she know that's not true. He come to her in a dream, you know; he tell her that bugger shot him. She never find his body.'

Sadie jumped as if she'd been bitten. 'What was his name?' she cried. 'Your uncle, was his name Jimmy Raven?'

Auntie Lily's mouth screwed up and her eyes narrowed as she peered toward Sadie. 'Who's that there?'

'Sadie Hazzard,' faltered Sadie.

'Huh.' Auntie Lily's milky eyes raked her up and down. 'You people, you think you know all about the Dreaming. You think the Dreaming was long, long ago. But you're wrong. The Dreaming is now. The Dreaming is always; forever; it circles around and around. It never ends. It's always happening, and us mob, we're part of it, all the time, everywhere, and every-*when* too. You think you know everything, but you don't understand. Everything's alive, not just people, not just animals; every rock, every tree. Do you know that?'

'I guess so,' whispered Sadie.

'Huh!' said Auntie Lily. 'You think you can hear all the secrets?'

Sadie knew there was no right answer to that question. She said nothing.

'Well, Sadie Hazzard, you go wait outside.'

The old woman drew herself upright and stared with her blinded eyes as Sadie backed miserably out of the room. She felt like crying. The crows had come to her; she hadn't asked them to choose her. This was her story, long before Walter arrived. Now Auntie Lily had shut her out. It wasn't fair.

She couldn't face slinking into the kitchen, filled and overflowing with the strong laughter of the women. They would probably despise her, too. Sadie slid down the wall of the hallway and sat on the thread-bare carpet.

Lily's uncle was Jimmy Raven; she was sure of it. And her auntie, Jimmy's wife, who'd seen him in a dream and searched for his body − what was her name?

'Netta,' whispered Sadie. 'It was Netta.'

Jimmy was the clever man, and something had been stolen from him. Gerald must have taken something from his body. His wallet? A key? It must be valuable, if the crows were so determined that it should be found. A watch, a ring, a medal? A paper with a secret? A will? A map? Sadie's head spun with possibilities.

After what seemed a long time, the door opened and Walter poked his head out. 'She wants you to come in again,' he said. Sadie scrambled up, and Walter laid his hand on her sleeve. 'You gotta under-stand – whitefellas have done lots of bad things in Auntie's life. It's hard for her to trust – someone like you.'

'But I'm not a bad person.'

'No one thinks they're a bad person,' said Walter. 'I'll bet even Gerald Mortlock didn't think he was a bad person. Just be careful with Auntie, that's all.'

Sadie edged into the darkened bedroom. Auntie Lily beckoned her close to the bed and grabbed her hand, as if to stop her from running away.

'Walter told me the crows talk to you. That true?'

Sadie nodded.

'And you seen my uncle?' Auntie's voice was stern.

Sadie lowered her eyes. 'Yes.'

'In a dream?'

Sadie hesitated. 'A kind of dream, I suppose. His name was Jimmy Raven. He got in a fight with – with another man. And his wife's name was Netta.'

Auntie Lily took in a long breath, and nodded. There was silence in the dim room. Sadie could hardly see Walter standing in the shadows.

'You got some blackfella blood in you?' Auntie Lily asked suddenly.

Sadie was startled. 'No.' Then, uncertainly, 'I don't think so. I don't know much about Dad's family. I don't know.'

'Huh,' said Auntie Lily.

There was a pause. At last the old lady said, 'You seen Crow's messengers. You seen my uncle. Walter says you can keep secrets. That right? Can you be trusted, Sadie Hazzard?'

Sadie felt a stab of guilt as she remembered how she'd betrayed Waa's place to Lachie. But she'd never do something like that again. She whispered, 'Yes. You can trust me.'

Auntie Lily shifted slightly on her pillows. Slowly, softly, she said, 'A clever man got special things, sacred, secret. He keeps them wrapped up, keeps them safe. No one allowed to see, no one allowed to touch. My Auntie Netta, she never could find out what happened to my uncle's special things. Maybe someone steal them, use the powers.' She shook her head. 'Bad luck from that.'

'It's breaking the Law,' said Sadie.

'That's right. That's right.'

'You think that's what the crows want us to find? Your uncle's special things?'

'Find his special things. Find his body, bury him proper. Take him back to his own country.' Auntie

Lily shrugged. 'I dunno what the spirits want. You the ones who talk to the crows, eh, you the ones they talk to.' She dropped back suddenly against her pillows, and fluttered her hand to dismiss them. 'I'm tired now.'

'Auntie?' said Walter. 'Can't you tell us what they are, the secret special things? Only it's going to make it hard to look for them, if we don't know what they are.'

Auntie shook her head, her eyes closed. 'Maybe them crows, they tell you. Maybe you have another dream. Maybe you see my uncle again, watch him good. Maybe that man who killed him, he take them away. You watch and see.'

'Thank you, Auntie,' said Walter. 'Thanks for talking to us.'

'Thanks, Auntie,' Sadie managed to say. She sidled to the door.

Walter lingered by the bed. 'And if we do find them, should we bring them to you?'

Auntie Lily's eyes snapped open. 'Don't you kids go poking at them secret things,' she said sharply. 'Not for you to look at. You bring them straight to me, wrapped up good. Not for me to look at, neither. But I know the right person to give them to. You bring them to me.'

'We promise,' said Walter. He backed out of the room and joined Sadie in the hallway, closing the door softly behind them. He muttered, 'Only we're never gonna find them. How can we find them when we don't even know what they are?'

Sadie caught his arm. 'But we can – maybe I can. Didn't you hear what she said? I can find out. I can go back to 1933, back to that night. It's the only way.'

Walter considered. 'But you can't *decide* to go back, can you? You can't click your fingers and go. Every other time you kind of fell into it; you didn't control it.'

Sadie's face fell. 'Yeah,' she said slowly. 'I guess so.'

'I reckon the Mortlocks have got them,' Walter said, low and fierce.

Sadie stared at him. 'Yeah?'

'Yeah. That's why they had bad luck. Gerald Mortlock died, didn't he? And his dam dried up, and their creek, and they've got no money, and Lachie's a dickhead, and his dad's a dickhead too.'

Sadie couldn't help giggling. Then she said softly, 'But the Hazzards had bad luck, too...Clarry and Sadie died as well...'

Walter shook his head. 'I reckon Gerald Mortlock stole them off Jimmy that night. It makes sense, doesn't it?'

Sadie gasped, and clutched Walter's arm. 'Craig said the other day that he had some Aboriginal bits and pieces lying around—'

They stared at each other.

'They got them in that big old house,' Walter said, 'hidden away somewhere.'

'So what are we going to do?'

Walter drew himself upright. 'Easy. Go and take them back.'

They had to wait a week, until Saturday, when Craig and Amanda and Lachie would all be at the football. Bethany had gone back to university; Walter heard Lachie telling someone in the corridor at school. Not so long ago, Sadie would have envied Bethany that long trip back to the city, but not now.

'You guys not coming?' Ellie raised her eyebrows. '*Again*? Not interested in the triumphant march of the Magpies into the finals? You realise if we beat Donald today, Boort will actually be in the semis next week?'

Walter shrugged and stared at the carpet.

'We've got stuff to do,' said Sadie. 'We need to work on that project.'

David put his arm round Ellie. 'They'll be all right. Leave them to it, eh?'

'We don't have much time,' warned Sadie, as the door shut behind Ellie and David. 'The game'll be over in a couple of hours.'

Walter slung a backpack over his shoulder. 'Better get moving.'

Sadie locked the door and dropped the key into her pocket, and they set off, heading inland, across the railway tracks, away from the town and the Little Lake, toward the Invergarry homestead.

'Any crows talk to you this week?' said Walter. 'They give you any more clues?'

Sadie shook her head. Walter began to whistle between his teeth, a monotonous insect whine like a miniature trail bike.

'Stop it,' said Sadie.

Walter stopped.

After a pause, Sadie said, 'Are you nervous?'

'Nah,' said Walter. He jammed his fists into his pockets. He was walking so fast Sadie could hardly keep up.

'What's in the bag?' she panted.

'Nothing,' said Walter. 'Yet.'

Sadie had a few moments of panic when she thought they'd taken the wrong road. She'd checked the map, but had forgotten to bring it with her. *She* was scared, even if Walter wasn't. Breaking into other people's houses wasn't the way she normally spent a Saturday afternoon... Maybe it would be a good thing if they *were* lost. Then they could go home, or go and watch the footy after all, have a sausage in bread and cheer on the Magpies.

She was almost disappointed when they reached the gate, with its crooked sign announcing *Invergarry*, and a battered milk can for a mailbox.

They stood by the side of the road, staring at the sign.

'What if they're home?' said Sadie. 'What if they haven't gone to the game after all?'

Walter shrugged. 'Say you've come to visit Lachie.' He looked at her sideways. 'You guys are kind of friendly.'

Sadie was stung. 'Not *now*. Not since they yelled at us. Not since they wiped their boots on the stones. Not since they shot the crows.' Listing the Mortlocks' crimes fired her resolve, and she grabbed the top of the gate and clambered over. 'Come on.'

Walter landed with a thud beside her. A deeply rutted dirt track unspooled from the gate, stretching between flat paddocks dotted with grey sheep.

'Pretty long driveway, hey,' said Walter after fifteen minutes.

Sadie quickened her pace. Surely they must come to the house soon; they couldn't have missed it. But the track seemed to go on forever, a salmon-coloured ribbon winding through the scrubby grass.

At last they came over a shallow rise, and the homestead was revealed on the crest of the next hill: a square, grey box, surrounded by lawns and flowering shrubs, a splash of lush green in the midst of yellow-grey paddocks. A small dam nearby was ringed with eucalypts, their trunks gnarled and twisted, their frayed crowns whispering in the breeze. A flock of cockatoos wheeled across the winter blue, their wings dazzling white in the sun, and disappeared over the horizon.

It was so beautiful. And the Mortlocks owned it all, further than the eye could see. Maybe if this was her backyard, she'd want to protect it, too.

Walter scanned the area outside the house. 'No cars,' he said. 'No one home.'

He broke into a trot as he set off down the gentle slope, his bag swaying on his back.

The garden was surrounded by a low stone wall with a wooden gate. Walter lifted the latch.

'What are you *doing*?' said Sadie.

'Gotta check no one's home.' He marched up to the front door and buzzed.

Sadie's heart hammered as they waited in the silence; but no one came.

'Okay,' said Walter. 'Now we go round the back.'

They flitted around the side of the house. Walter peered through the glass in the kitchen door. 'Can't see anyone.' He moved from one window to the next, trying each sash in turn. At last he gave Sadie a thumbs-up. He'd managed to shift one up a few centimetres. 'Gimme that box; I need something to stand on.'

'This is burgling,' said Sadie. But she fetched the box.

'Not if they leave the window open.'

'I don't think that's right,' said Sadie doubtfully.

Walter climbed onto the box and gave the window a good shove. With a creak of protest, it slid up. Walter pulled himself onto the sill and wriggled inside. There was a loud thump and some swearing.

Sadie hugged her hands beneath her armpits and glanced around anxiously until Walter's curly head reappeared.

'Easy,' he said. 'I'll open the back door for you.'

A minute later, Sadie tiptoed into the Mortlocks' kitchen. It was vast and old and lined with crooked cupboards. A long wooden table ran down the middle of the room, heaped with papers and fruit bowls and a pair of shoes that someone hadn't finished cleaning. Little rooms led off in all directions – a walk-in pantry; a funny little room with a sink and haphazard shelves stacked with crockery; a space crowded with boots and hats and coats and umbrellas; a glassed-in verandah. Everything was still and musty and cold, but scrupulously clean. Pictures hung on faded wallpaper. Shabby roses on the carpet had been almost trodden away. The canvas backing showed along the centre of the hallway.

'Where do you reckon we ought to look?' Walter's voice was hushed.

'How should I know?' Sadie shivered. Though the house was empty, she felt as if a crowd of ghosts were watching her. She walked down the hall, peering through doorways. The first room held a TV, leather couches, trophies on the mantelpiece, school photos of Bethany with her two blonde pony-tails, and Lachie, freckle-faced and hair sticking out. Sadie ducked out of the room, feeling embarrassed.

In the next room, a sewing machine sat on a bench under the window, neatly folded bolts of fabric were arranged on shelves, and a naked dressmaker's dummy stood by the door.

'Nothing there,' said Sadie in a hushed voice. Her toes curled inside her shoes. The longer they stayed there, the deeper they crept into the house, the more convinced she was that this was a mistake.

Walter called softly from further down the hall-way. 'In here.'

He'd found a room with a huge fireplace and a pool table, overhung with fringed lights. The room was as dark and hushed as a church, the walls lined with sepia photographs in heavy wooden frames.

There was a photo of two soldiers posing stiffly in uniform. There was a bridal couple, the man's face half-hidden by a moustache, the bride in a froth of creamy lace, clutching her bouquet under her chin and looking scared. A family group stared solemnly at the camera, the baby just a blur where he'd wriggled at the wrong moment. A gold-edged diploma from the Tonic Sol-Fa School of Vocal Music, for Felicity Mortlock. A medal with a letter signed by George V, thanking Edwin Mortlock for dying for the Empire. A medal for George Mortlock, elaborately framed and mounted – For Acts of Gallantry and Devotion to Duty Under Fire. A map of Invergarry, showing the dams and the homestead and the Boort road – Lake Invergarry was shaded in blue. It was the history of a family, generation after generation, ranged on the walls.

But the room didn't tell the whole truth. Sadie knew that. Beneath the proud photos and the certificates lay shame, and stories never told. Where was Gerald Mortlock? Where was the Raven family, who'd lived and died here, too? And beneath that lay yet another layer of history, deep and still as rock, alive as the land itself ...

Walter breathed, 'Here.'

Sadie joined him before a glass case in a corner of the room. Two stuffed wallabies gazed mutely, miserably, back at them. A set of labelled rocks. A piece of coral ringed with cowry shells. The bleached skull of a bird. A pipe and a black silk tobacco pouch.

Sadie whispered, 'Those belonged to Mr Mortlock ... Gerald Mortlock, I mean.'

Walter pointed with a shaking hand.

Right at the back of the cabinet, almost invisible in the shadows, was a pile of bones.

A shock like an electric jolt ran through Sadie's body. Without intending to, she groped for Walter's hand, and he gripped hers, both of them mute with horror.

'What are you doing here?'

Lachie stood in the doorway, his fair hair tousled, his blue eyes blazing. He snapped on the lights, and Sadie and Walter flinched from the sudden glare.

Sadie faltered, 'We were just – looking.'

'How did you get in here?' Lachie stalked forward. Sadie shrank back, but Walter stood his ground.

'The back door was open,' he said defiantly. 'Go and look, it's open.'

'Yeah, it's open *now*,' said Lachie. 'But I didn't leave it open. I locked it up myself. Came back to get my footy boots and I find a couple of dirty little thieves have broken in.'

'We're not thieves,' said Sadie. Her tongue felt thick inside her mouth.

'Liar,' said Lachie.

Sadie saw his eyes flick to Walter's hand clutching hers. She gripped Walter's hand even tighter and stared back at Lachie.

'We didn't touch nothing,' said Walter.

'Because I got here in time to stop you clearing the place out,' said Lachie. 'You think the police are going to believe you?'

Walter caught his breath. He muttered, 'No need for that, mate.'

'I'm not your mate, *mate*.'

'You think this is going to make you look tough?' said Sadie, shrilly. 'You think your dad'll be impressed? You think Nank and Hammer and Troy and Jules will think you're a hero? Me and Walter aren't exactly armed robbers.'

Lachie blinked, then recovered. 'Doesn't matter. You're still criminals.'

Sadie flung out a finger to point behind her. 'Where did those bones come from?'

Lachie screwed up his face. 'I dunno. A kangaroo or something. Who cares?' He took another step forward. 'You better start thinking about what you're going to tell Brad Ringrose down at the police station. Better think about calling your lawyer, *mate*.'

Quick as the flash of a lizard's tongue, Walter moved. He shot round the other side of the pool table and darted for the door, yanking Sadie with him. Lachie dived sideways and grabbed at Sadie's jacket, but with a desperate wrench she wriggled free and pelted down the hallway after Walter. Lachie hurtled after them. Sadie and Walter skidded across the linoleum floor of the kitchen and flung themselves at the open door, at the square of cool air, at freedom.

'**R**un, run!' yelled Walter. He let go of Sadie's hand and they raced across the yard. A dog began to bark wildly; they veered away from the sound, away from the farm buildings, sprinting in the opposite direction from the way they'd come, weaving between the gum trees and across the paddock.

Sadie's heart drummed in her ears, a stitch burned her side. She looked back. 'He's not following us!'

Walter slowed down, glanced over his shoulder. 'Oh, yes, he is.'

And then Sadie heard it too: the whine of the trail bike.

'Split up!' Walter shouted, but they kept running side by side, racing across the hill. A wire fence loomed ahead and Sadie slid to a halt – what if it was electric? But there were no warning signs, and Walter was already scrambling through.

'This'll slow him down,' he panted, and Sadie nodded, tangled in the wire; she had no breath to reply. She wriggled through to the other side, and then they were off again, running until it seemed their lungs would burst.

Behind them, the angry buzz of the trail bike rose and fell. Sadie's frantic gaze swept the horizon. Where were they running to? Deeper and deeper into Invergarry, deeper into Lachie's territory? She wished she could remember the map. Her breath tore in her chest.

Wah! Wah!

High overhead, the black dot of a crow circled in the pale blue sky.

Sadie threw up her hands. 'Help! Crows, help us!'

Wah! Wah! The crow's cries were sharp and harsh. It glided nearer, and dipped its wings like a signal.

'Walter! This way!' Sadie shouted, and stumbled after the big black bird. The noise of the trail bike grew louder; it was getting closer.

The crow wheeled above them, cawing. Its cries could have been a warning or a command. Sadie ran on blindly, letting the crow lead her. Suddenly she realised they were headed for the dry lake. She'd never approached it from this side. But there was the caked yellow sediment, flaking in the sun like the scales of some prehistoric beast. And now she knew where they were running to, where the crow was taking them.

Waah-waaah.

The crow gave a cry of satisfaction and swooped down to perch on one of the stones in the ring. It folded its wings and stared at Sadie with a glittering eye as she ran, panting, down the slope of the hidden valley. She stopped herself just outside the circle. 'Can I? Are we allowed?'

The crow inclined its head, giving permission, and Sadie threw herself inside the shelter of the stones. She called to Walter, 'We'll be safe now!'

Walter flung himself into the circle, and bent to catch his breath. 'You kidding? We're not safe here. He's still coming.'

They couldn't see Lachie, but the drone of the bike was louder than ever.

'This is Waa's place,' said Sadie. 'The crows will protect us—'

Walter shook his head. 'Lachie doesn't think this is a magic place. It won't work…'

The bike's engine revved and snarled, and suddenly the bike itself flew over the top of a ridge and roared down onto the lake bed, spraying yellow mud.

Waah! Waah!

One, two, three more crows fluttered down to perch on top of the stones. Sadie swung round. Every stone in the circle was crowned with a sleek black bird; more crows flapped overhead, cawing. She gripped Walter's arm.

'See? I told you they'd look after us!'

The bike roared up. The sun glinted on Lachie's hair; he hadn't stopped to put on his helmet. He halted the bike about fifty metres away and revved the engine.

'What's he going to do?' muttered Walter.

'He can't do anything!' said Sadie. 'He can't get us now! The crows are guarding us.'

Walter squinted across the lake bed. 'We're trapped here.'

'It's okay,' said Sadie. 'He'll go, he'll leave.'

But even as she spoke, Lachie revved the engine to a deafening roar, and drove the bike straight at the stone circle. Sadie screamed, Walter yelped, and they jumped back, pressing themselves flat against the rocks.

'What's he doing?' shrieked Sadie.

'Trying to kill us!' shouted Walter.

But Lachie wasn't going fast; he edged the bike forward, nosing it toward the rocks as if he meant to guide it right inside the circle. Then at the last instant he nudged the bike against one of the sacred stones. He drew back and butted the rock again. It wobbled.

'He's trying to knock them down!' Sadie screamed.

The crows rose in a cloud, flapping and cawing, and circled above the ring. 'Stop him!' shrieked Sadie. 'Can't you stop him?' If only the crows would fly at Lachie, attack him, make him stop!

Again Lachie drew the bike back, and again drove it forward. There was another sickening crunch as the front tyre knocked the tall stone off-balance. It lurched sideways, and Lachie hastily revved his engine and retreated out of the way. But the stone didn't fall. Lachie spun the bike, spraying an arc of yellow mud high behind him. He lined up the bike again to take another run at the unsteady rock.

'*Stop it!*' screamed Sadie.

Beside her, Walter stooped, and threw something.

The clod of dried mud shattered as it hit Lachie on the arm. He shouted out in shock. The bike slewed from under him on the slippery surface, and crashed over, flinging Lachie sideways. The bike's wheels spun, spitting pellets of mud into the air. The crows sent up a deafening, discordant chorus, their cries of *wah! wah!* overlapping in a panicked din.

Lachie lay on the ground, unmoving.

Sadie broke out of the circle and flung herself down beside him. Blood trickled down his face; his eyes were closed. He'd been thrown clear of the bike, which still roared and bellowed like a wounded creature a few metres away. 'Lachie? Lachie?'

'Oh my God.' Walter hugged his arms round himself, his face ashen. 'I didn't mean it. Is he dead? Is he dead or what?'

'He's hit his head on a rock, I think.' Sadie felt sick. Blood was pooling beneath Lachie's head, matting his hair. The memory of Jimmy Raven flashed into her mind, the sticky blood, the dreadful weight of his dying, and for an instant the world shimmered, wobbling like the dislodged stone. The two times blurred, between Sadie now and Sadie then, between Jimmy's body and Lachie's, between the darkness and the day. She lowered her head as the light throbbed and the crows' cries echoed around her.

Walter grabbed her shoulder. 'Sadie, we got to get out of here!'

Shock returned her to herself. '*What?* We've got to help him!'

'What do you want to do, carry him back to town?' shouted Walter. 'It's gotta be an accident; we got nothing to do with it. If he's hurt bad, if he dies – if they find out we were in his house, if they find out I chucked something at him – oh man. Oh God.'

Gerald Mortlock's voice echoed in Sadie's head. *It was an accident, I swear to God!* The same panic, the same despair...

Was it the same story, playing itself out again? Was it her fault? She couldn't let the same thing happen again...

Walter sank to his knees on the yellow mud and buried his head in his arms. 'You don't know what'll happen to me. They'll send me away. They'll lock me up. I'm on my last chance.' He raised his head and stared at Sadie with haunted eyes. 'If they lock me up again I'll kill myself.'

'We can't leave him here!' Sadie was weeping. 'If we leave him here, he *will* die!' She tried to lift Lachie's head. He moaned, his face drained of colour.

The story tells itself again...

The three of them were in the grip of Crow's story, just as Gerald and Clarry and Jimmy had been. But Crow couldn't see, Crow couldn't help them. Sadie was the only one who knew; it was all up to her.

The world spun before her eyes. She tried to say, 'Walter – you can't – we have to—' But her voice clogged in her throat, as if the yellow mud choked her. The crows shrieked overhead, their calls rose and fell as their wings sliced the air like razors.

Black filled the sky; black filled Sadie's eyes.

She heard Walter cry her name, very far away, but she was falling down a tunnel and everything was black.

'Sadie!'

Dad was shaking her shoulder.

'Sadie, come on, love. I need you now.'

She nodded dumbly, clutching at the edge of the shop counter. The shop tilted and swayed around her like a merry-go-round, but she took a deep breath and the world firmed and steadied.

Mr Mortlock had sagged across the counter, limp as a rag doll. 'Thank God!' he muttered. 'I knew I could count on you, Clarry.'

Dad's face was expressionless. He bent and picked up the bundle of bloodied clothes that Mr Mortlock had left on the floor, and bunched them in his hands. 'I'll get rid of these,' he said. 'You should go.'

Mr Mortlock picked up his hat. Silently he held out his hand, and after a moment, Clarry shook it.

Clarry said in a low voice, 'Are we square?'

'We're square,' said Mr Mortlock.

They didn't look at each other.

Sadie watched the two men as if they were figures at the wrong end of a telescope; they seemed tiny, diminished, hardly worth hating.

Mr Mortlock touched the brim of his hat and slipped out of the shop. Dad bolted the door behind him. He stood with his back to Sadie.

'Seen worse things in France,' he said. He glanced round, and there was a plea in his eyes; Sadie realised with a shock that he wanted her forgiveness.

She couldn't give it. She dropped her gaze. She was numb inside.

After a moment, Dad cleared his throat. 'I'd better put these in the stove.'

Sadie found her voice. 'No. I'll do it.' She held out her hand. 'And your clothes will need washing.'

'Don't show your mother.'

'No. I won't.'

She met his eyes then, and the look that passed between them was a promise. Sadie watched as her father shuffled out of the shop. He seemed to have aged a hundred years in a single night. She knew that she would never see him in the same way again; something had shifted between them. Never again would her father be her rescuer, her protector, all-powerful and wise. He had lost his authority forever. Now Sadie would be the one to protect Clarry.

She took the bundle of Gerald Mortlock's ruined clothes into the kitchen and poked them into the stove's mouth. Flames flared, and shadows danced along the walls. In the hiss and crackle of the fire, Sadie thought she heard the sounds of mourning; she thought she heard wails and sobbing, and outside in the night, she heard an owl cry and the distant voice of a crow.

Waaah...waaah...

Dad had crept into the kitchen behind her. He was wearing his pyjamas; mutely he held out his own filthy clothes to Sadie. She stood and took them from him.

'You go to bed,' she told him. 'Is Mum asleep?'

He nodded. 'Thanks, love,' he croaked, and coughed into his sleeve.

'Go to bed,' she said again, and watched him shuffle away, stooped and broken, an old man.

In the flickering half-light from the open stove, her mind far away, Sadie reached into the pockets of her father's trousers, as her mother always did before the wash. Automatically she emptied coins and keys and lengths of string from one pocket onto the table, then reached her hand into the other.

Her fingers touched soft fur. At the same instant, the crow cried outside. Sadie snatched her hand back as though she'd touched the hot stove.

Then, slowly, she drew out a small bundle, wrapped in what looked like possum fur. She had a confused impression of small shifting objects beneath her fingertips before she dropped the bundle on the tabletop. A kind of horror, a kind of fear, ran through her like a shudder. It was the package that Jimmy had handed to her father before he died.

Burn it, said a voice inside her head.

And another voice, a voice that was and was not her own, cried out, *No!*

The fire sputtered and flared; shadows wheeled across the ceiling like swooping birds. Two worlds, two selves, struggled inside Sadie's mind, pushing against each other like two magnets.

Then, abruptly, she knew she was Sadie – Sadie out of time, Ellie Hazzard's daughter, Sadie from the future. She stood in the strange kitchen, in the flickering dark, and she was afraid. But she knew why she was here; she knew what she had to do.

With shaking hands, she took the Blue Crane cigarette tin from her cardigan pocket – from the other Sadie's pocket – and wrenched off the lid. Gingerly she picked up Jimmy's precious bundle, his sacred objects wrapped in fur, and squashed them down inside the tin and pushed on the lid. She stood for a moment, pressing the tin between her hands.

She couldn't let the other Sadie destroy these things. To Jimmy, to his people, they were holy objects, magical objects, filled with mysterious power. It would be as awful, as disrespectful, as melting down the communion cup or the crucifix from the other Sadie's church.

She pushed the tin back into her pocket. It dragged there, too heavy for what was inside it. It weighed like lead.

She took Clarry's clothes out to the lean-to. She found a tin tub, half-full of water, with clothes already soaking, and she shoved Clarry's shirt and trousers in among them.

She stood in the cold air, in the darkness. A single light shone from above the pub; as she watched, it was extinguished. What time was it? The tin burned cold under her hand.

Stars salted the sky overhead. Sadie began to walk, quickly, stumbling not up the main street but across the road and along the railway track, circling away from the few houses nearby, turning her back to the town. She pushed her way into the scrub that fringed the lake, into the bush. She swapped the tin from hand to hand, felt it bruising her palms.

It was too dark to see properly; branches scraped and scratched her. She thought of Jimmy lying lonely in the cold ground with no one to say goodbye; dirt scraped over him like a dead dog. He was far from his own country, lying in strange ground. Now he could never go home.

Tears leaked down Sadie's cheeks. A crow called, and she followed the sound, pushing blindly through the bush. She stumbled and caught onto a tree trunk to save herself. *Waah!* called the crow. *Here.*

She wound her hand around the smooth, slender trunk. It was a gum tree sapling, young and pure and perfect.

Sadie fell to her knees and scrabbled at the dirt beneath the tree with her bare hands. Soon her fingers closed around a short, stout stick and she began to dig with that. The digging soothed her; it was a job to do. The earth was soft and damp. The sapling seemed to bend over her watchfully, its leafy fingers caressing her hair. She heard the tiny noises of the bush night: scampering paws, rustling grasses, the soft sad hoot of a mopoke, the mournful hum of the frogs. The night was alive, it belonged to itself. It was a separate world, as different from the world of day as the old world was different from the new. The day might belong to the other Sadie's God, the God of churches; but the night belonged to ancient, nameless gods, to silent spirits, to Waa and Bunjil and all the others. Sadie dug into the earth, she made a hole in the body of the land, and as she dug, she whispered, 'I'm sorry, I'm so sorry.'

When the hole was deep enough, she placed the tin at the bottom. She covered it over with earth as reverently as if it were Jimmy Raven's body she buried there. The other Sadie would have said a prayer; but Sadie didn't know any.

When the hole was filled, she pressed her hands down flat upon the spot and bowed her head. She felt the cold eyes of the stars stare down at her; the icy fingers of the night mist wreathed around her legs. She realised she was chilled to the bone; the thin cardigan wasn't enough to protect her.

Stiffly she clambered up, and turned to go. But suddenly panic seized her. This sapling, among all the saplings in the bush – she'd never find it again. What if – What if—

She dropped to her knees at the foot of the young tree once more, and scrabbled in the dirt and the litter of fallen leaves until her hand closed over a stone. Laboriously she scraped at the base of the trunk, carving an S, a snake-shaped scar, into the bark. S for Sadie, S for secret, for stones, sacred stone, S for sorry. She let the stone fall and staggered to her feet.

I'm delirious, she thought. *I'm getting a fever.* A violent shudder racked her body, and a chill sweat broke out all over her skin. She stumbled through the bush, dropping one foot in front of the other with no idea which way she was walking. *I'm lost*, she thought at last. *If I stay out here all night, I'm done for.*

Clarry wouldn't come looking for her; he didn't know where she was, he was probably asleep by now. No one knew where she was. Dad would need help to find her. Jimmy Raven was the best tracker in the district...

But Jimmy was dead.

Sadie stumbled and fell. She rolled over and stared up at the tangled trees, silvered by the starlight, and another violent shiver shook her from head to foot. She would lie here for a little while to rest and catch her strength. Then she'd find her way home.

She felt herself slipping out of the other Sadie's mind, and the other Sadie seeped back into her own body, like dye curling through water.

She closed her eyes, and the dark rolled over her like a tide.

'Sadie! Sadie! Wake up!'

Sadie blinked. Walter's anxious face stared down at her.

'You okay?' He helped her to sit up.

Lachie was still sprawled in the dirt. The trail bike sputtered feebly on its side. She must have only fainted for a minute, though she felt as if she'd been away for hours.

Sadie clutched at Walter as she hauled herself to her feet. 'We've got to help him.' She pointed to the bike. 'Can you ride it?'

Walter blinked. 'I dunno. I can try.' He looked at the bike, then at Lachie. 'All right, I'll go and get help. You stay with Lachie, yeah?'

'Okay.' Sadie hugged her arms around herself.

Waaa-aaah...waaa-aaah...

A melancholy drawl signalled the agreement of a distant crow. Walter pushed his fingers through his hair. Then he jogged to the fallen bike, heaved it upright, and slung his leg over the seat. The engine growled, the bike jerked, and Walter almost lost his balance – then he was off. Sadie waved frantically as the bike roared away. She had a last glimpse of Walter's face, scowling with concentration, as he disappeared across the lake bed, trailing plumes of yellow mud in his wake. The whine of the bike faded and there was silence.

Sadie knelt beside Lachie and lifted his head onto her lap. He groaned, his eyes squeezed shut. She wriggled out of her jacket and wrapped it around his head like a bandage, pulling it tight to try to stop the bleeding.

'You're going to be all right, Lachie,' she said. She didn't know if he could hear her. She gripped his hand. 'Walter's gone to get help, they'll be here soon…' A terrible thought struck her. What if Walter didn't go to the oval? What if he just rode away?

'He'll be back soon…' she faltered.

Lachie moaned and tried to struggle up.

'Don't move!' cried Sadie. 'Keep still.' She squeezed his hand and thought of the other Sadie, lying in the bush, chilled through. Was that what made her sick, was that what killed her? Sadie shivered. Was that Crow's punishment?

And here she sat, with another man bleeding, in the same place, Crow's place... blood spilled on Crow's ground...

'It's different this time,' she said aloud, though she wasn't sure whether she spoke to herself, or Lachie or Waa, or to the crows who were Waa's messengers. 'Walter's getting help...'

She scanned the horizon for movement. What if Walter didn't come back? Already her jacket was soaked through with Lachie's blood. She remembered the blood on Gerald Mortlock's clothes, the blood on her fingers when she touched Jimmy's scalp.

She couldn't save Jimmy, but at least she'd saved his special things. And they would save Lachie...

'Hang on, Lachie,' she whispered. 'You can't die. It's got to be different this time.'

She looked around for a crow, hoping for some sign that Waa hadn't abandoned them. But the sky was empty, the stone circle sat silent. The lake bed stretched to the horizon, flat and blank and feature-less. She and Lachie were alone.

She didn't know how long she sat there with Lachie's head cradled in her lap. But at last there came a distant warning cry: *Waah! Waah! They are coming!*

She looked up. The murmur of engines drifted toward her from the edge of the lake. 'It's okay, Lachie!' she cried, almost weeping with relief. 'Walter's back! They're here!'

David put his arm around Sadie's shoulders as they watched Craig's 4WD bump away across the lake bed. Ellie was going with Lachie and his parents to the hospital; everyone else had drifted away, back to the pub, mostly. Boort had actually beaten Donald, even with the team one man short. It was the upset of the season, but no one cared about that now.

'Your mum said it's probably not as bad as it looks,' said David. 'Head wounds always bleed a lot. He'll probably be fine.' He looked across at Walter. 'I'm really proud of you two, reacting the way you did. It was quick thinking, taking the bike.'

Walter stared at the ground and mumbled something.

'I'm still not clear about exactly what happened.' David looked from Walter to Sadie. 'You just found Lachie here, did you? Lucky for him. Though it beats me what he was doing here. We sent him home for his footy boots; this isn't on the way...'

Walter cleared his throat. 'That's not—' He shot a desperate glance at Sadie. 'We didn't find him. He kind of found us.'

Sadie said nothing, though her insides twisted like a wet rag. It was up to Walter to decide how much to tell David. And up to David to decide what happened after that.

Walter lowered his head. 'We went to his house, the Mortlocks' house. Auntie Lily sent us to find some things, secret things.'

David's eyes narrowed. 'Auntie Lily told you to break into the Mortlocks' house?'

Walter shuffled miserably and said nothing.

'We didn't take anything,' said Sadie. 'Honest. We were only looking round.'

'But Lachie busted us. He chased after us – thought he was going to run us down.' Walter licked his lips. 'I mighta thrown something at him.'

'Only a lump of mud,' said Sadie. 'It wouldn't have hurt him. We didn't know he was going to fall off. We were scared. It was self-defence. It was an accident...' She let her voice trail away as she heard the echo of Gerald Mortlock's words.

David rubbed his hand over his face. He looked at Walter. 'What do you want to do?'

'It was my idea to go to the house,' said Walter slowly. 'I opened the window. And I knocked Lachie off his bike.'

The words weighed heavily in the silence. David waited. Sadie began to say, 'It was my fault, too—' but David held up a hand to quiet her.

Walter shrugged. 'I better go and see Lachie's mum and dad. Say sorry.'

'They might want to take it to the police,' said David.

'I know.'

David nodded. 'I'll be with you. We'll sort this out.'

He wrapped his arms around Walter, and they stood there, motionless, for a few moments. Sadie traced the cracks in the mud with her toe.

At last Walter said, 'It wasn't Sadie's fault. She just came along.'

'We did it together,' said Sadie hotly. 'All of it!' She wasn't going to let Walter take all the blame.

But at that moment, she heard the softest, most discreet *wah* from behind her, like a crow clearing its throat. And she remembered that she had another job to do.

David held out his hand. 'You coming?'

Sadie looked at Walter. 'I've got to do something for Auntie Lily. That special thing she asked us to find – I know where it is now.'

Walter's eyes lit up. 'You saw it?'

Sadie nodded.

'Tell me about it later,' said David. 'You'll be right to get home on your own, Sadie?'

Sadie pointed to the ring of stones. A crow was perched on top of one boulder, silently watching them.

'I won't be on my own,' she said. 'The crows will be with me.'

A frown crossed David's face, then he shrugged and laid his arm protectively across his nephew's shoulders. Sadie watched as they walked away across the yellow mud, then she turned to face the crow.

'I'm ready now,' she said.

The crow lifted its throat. '*Wah!*' It flapped down from the rock and looked expectantly at Sadie.

She set her face to the declining sun and followed the crow as it hopped across the lake bed, leading her where she needed to go.

27

The sapling had grown and spread into the old grey mallee gum in her own backyard.

Disbelieving, Sadie traced the S that she had carved into its trunk on that night so long ago, but only hours before. The scar was thickened and blurred, as high as her waist. She was sure she hadn't seen it there before.

When she'd carved her mark, the sapling was in the middle of the bush. In the years since, the houses had crept out from the centre of Boort and cleared the bush away. But the tree had survived.

The sky was clouding over as Sadie fetched Ellie's trowel from the shed. She didn't think she'd buried it very far down.

The crow watched her, its head tilted. When she poked the trowel into the earth, it hopped nearer, almost jabbing its beak into the hole. 'Look out,' said Sadie. 'Give me some room.'

The crow hopped back. '*Wah,*' it remarked.

Digging was harder work than Sadie had expected. The ground was dry and compacted; dirt crumbled into the hole she made. She kept striking roots and stones. As the hole grew larger with no sign of the buried tin she began to wonder if it was the wrong tree after all, or if someone else had found the tin before her. Her hair tumbled into her eyes and she pushed it back impatiently, leaving smudges of dirt across her face.

She wondered if Lachie was all right. She wondered if Craig and Amanda would be very angry with Walter. She wondered when Ellie would come home.

'You seek what was stolen,' said the crow beside her.

'I think it's here,' said Sadie. 'I think I can find it.'

The crow's mad eye regarded her with glittering excitement; it shifted restlessly from foot to foot. 'What was stolen must be restored.'

Sadie sat back on her heels. 'Everything that was stolen can't be given back,' she said. 'The land, the stories. The lives that were ended.'

'*Waah!* Life does not end. Life returns to Crow, to the ancestors. There is no ending.'

Sadie turned back to her digging. The sun was going down, the air was chilly. She thrust the trowel into the ground and it jarred against something hard. Sadie poked and scraped. Was it another rock? Her heart beat fast when she saw a metallic gleam at the bottom of the hole.

'*Wah! Wah!*' The crow flapped its wings and jigged up and down as Sadie tugged the tin from the earth where it had been buried so long. 'It is found!'

Sadie set the tin on the ground and stared at it. In the other Sadie's time, it had been fresh and new, with smart black paint and gilt edging, the label with its blue crane bright and glowing. Now the tin was rusty, battered, filthy. But it had guarded Jimmy Raven's secret possessions safely. Sadie remembered Auntie Lily's warning; she wouldn't open it.

'Now I have to give it to Auntie Lily,' Sadie said. 'That's right, isn't it?'

'To the elders, to the guardians. *Wah!*' The crow flapped its wings. Its eyes shone like black diamonds.

Sadie wrapped her palms around the tin. It was heavy; she remembered that unnatural heaviness from the other Sadie's time, as if the whole weight of a family's grief was enclosed within it.

'I wish I knew where Jimmy's body was buried,' she said. 'I wish I could tell Auntie Lily where he is.'

The crow's head cocked to one side. 'The bones of the clever man lie in Crow's country. We will find them. But first you must take the power to the elders.'

Sadie scrambled to her feet, clutching the tin with both hands. 'Auntie Lily, right – Oh!' She realised she couldn't remember the way to Auntie Lily and Vonn's house. She slumped against the tree, feeling the rough scratch of the bark at her back, fighting tears. She was tired and cold, her whole body ached with weariness. 'I don't know where to go,' she said dully.

'*Wah!*' cawed the crow, and spread its wings as it laughed at her. 'I will show you.'

The crow hopped from roof to roof, from tree to tree, leading her on through the town, past the RSL hall, the bowling club and the service station, out along the Boort–Yando road. Sadie trudged numbly through the dusk, her face nipped by the frosty air, her hands thrust into her pockets. The cold metal of the too-heavy tin burned through the fabric of her jacket and bit against her thigh.

'*Wah!*' the crow encouraged her. 'Come! Come!'

And it seemed to Sadie that the other birds were gathering by the roadside, a trio of magpies, a pair of galahs, a chattering flock of tiny green parrots, all watching as she passed. The road stretched before her.

'*Waah!*' called the crow. 'Here!'

The crow led Sadie around to the backyard of Auntie Vonn's house. A washing-line draped with sheets was strung between her and the back door. Lights glowed in the windows.

'She is there,' said the crow. 'The one you call Auntie Lily. Crow knows her by another name. Give her what you've found.' It hopped from foot to foot. 'Finish your story.'

Sadie hesitated. 'Will I speak to you again?' she asked shyly.

The crow opened its beak wide and laughed its cawing laugh. '*Wa-wa-waaah!* You may speak to us every day if you wish it. Isn't this Crow's country?'

Still laughing, it spread its wings and leaped into the air, a black shadow circling overhead. There was a rush of wind against Sadie's face as its wings beat the air. And then it was gone.

Sadie stood in the shadows by the back step for a few moments, listening to the laughter and music coming from the kitchen. She knocked on the door. 'Hello?' But no one heard her.

She pushed at the door, and it creaked open. 'Hello?' she called again, advancing into the house. She clutched the tin in her pocket between both her hands, as if it might give her courage.

A woman came rushing round the corner and almost knocked Sadie off her feet. 'Who's this?' she exclaimed. 'You nearly gave me a heart attack!'

The woman propelled Sadie into the light, and Sadie saw that it was Vonn. Recognition dawned in Vonn's face. 'You came with David and Walter, didn't you?' She sent a puzzled glance over Sadie's shoulder, out into the night. 'They here too?'

Sadie shook her head. 'I've come to see Auntie Lily,' she whispered. 'I've brought her something. It's important.'

Vonn's broad face softened. 'Auntie Lily's not well, darling. You give me whatever it is; I'll pass it on, eh?'

Sadie shook her head and gripped the tin tightly. It burned her fingers. 'I have to give it to Auntie Lily. No one else.'

Vonn looked her up and down, taking in the smears of dirt on Sadie's face, the splashes of blood on her clothes, the yellow mud that clung to her shoes.

'Please!' begged Sadie. 'Auntie told me to come.'

Vonn seemed to make up her mind. 'You come in here.' She thrust Sadie into the crowded kitchen. Startled faces turned to them. 'Jarred, get off that chair, let Sadie sit down. Look at her, she's that tired out, she can hardly stand up. You want a cup of tea, darling? Chrissie, you make her a cup of tea, or a Milo, eh? You sit down, Sadie. I'll go and see if Auntie's awake.'

Sadie sank into a chair and stared at her hands. She hadn't realised how tired she was until Vonn said it, but now exhaustion threatened to crash over her like an avalanche. Someone pushed a mug of steaming Milo in front of her and she curled her hands around it. 'Thanks,' she managed to whisper. Gradually the conversation picked up again, and soon it was swirling over and around her as if she wasn't there. She was grateful; she wished she could disappear, melt into nothing, the way the crow had dissolved into the night…

Vonn returned. 'Auntie wants to see you.' She ushered Sadie down the hall, and Sadie folded her hands around the tin and hugged it to her as she stepped into Auntie's room.

A bedside lamp in a ruffled shade cast a pink pool of light over the bed. Auntie was propped on pillows, a red knitted cardigan pulled around her shoulders. She patted the bed for Sadie to come nearer.

'You got something for me?'

Sadie edged closer to the bed. She pulled out the battered cigarette tin – heavy, so much heavier than it should be – and held it out. 'I found it. His special things, the secret things. They're in there.'

'You looked?' Auntie's voice was sharp.

Sadie shook her head. 'I just know.' She set the tin down on the flowery bedspread.

Auntie's wrinkled hand reached out to curve around it. 'Good girl.' She let out a deep sigh. 'Go on, you go. I look after this now.'

'Thanks,' said Sadie awkwardly, and shuffled backwards out of the room.

Vonn was waiting in the hallway. 'All done?'

Sadie nodded. She was so tired suddenly that she couldn't speak.

'You want to go home now?' suggested Vonn. 'Want me to ring someone, your mum, maybe? Or David?'

Sadie slumped against the wall as she recited Ellie's mobile number. She was dimly aware of Vonn speaking, making reassuring noises into the phone. She slid down the wall and leaned her head against a bookcase. As if in a dream, she saw Vonn bend down beside her and explain that her mum and David were on their way. 'From the hospital, yeah? That sound right? They'll be here soon.'

Sadie nodded, laboriously, because her head had grown so heavy, as heavy as the cigarette tin... She jolted awake. The tin, she had to deliver it to Auntie!

Then she remembered that she'd already done it. She'd done what the crows had wanted; it was all over. And then holding her head up was really too hard, and keeping her eyelids open was impossible.

Even when David and Ellie swooped into the house, even when David scooped her up and carried her to the car, she didn't wake. She was dreaming of a flight beneath the stars; she dreamed it all the way home.

She was leaning forward along the neck of a giant crow, her hands buried in its feathers. The freezing wind stung her face and hands. Far below, the land spread out beneath them, dots of light twinkled against the darkened earth, like a reflection of the star-sprinkled canopy of the sky above.

The steady *whoosh* of the crow's wings was the only sound as the spirit-bird flew across the darkness, a needle through the night. Silver clouds shredded to reveal the shining face of the full moon.

And Sadie knew that she was gazing down at ancient campfires, lit by the people of Crow and Eaglehawk, night after night, generation after generation, millennium upon millennium; that the time of electric lights was only a blink in the long dream of this land's story. The secret magic of this country lay hidden, buried under buildings and blood; but it had never gone away, and it would never disappear. It lay waiting, lost in its own endless dream.

'Tell Waa!' Sadie shouted. 'Tell him his stories aren't forgotten! His people remember; his people are still here! You have to tell him! It's important!'

'*Waah!* Crow knows this. Crow says—' But the next words were stolen by the wind, and all Sadie heard was the crow's cawing laughter.

Ellie tucked Sadie into bed without undressing her, dropped a kiss on her forehead and smoothed her hair. Something tangled in Ellie's fingers. Puzzled, she held it up to the light.

It was a black feather.

Ellie laid it on the bedside table and tiptoed from the room.

S adie and Walter walked across the dry lake bed.
'You think we'll be able to find it?' said Walter.
It was the first time either of them had spoken
since they'd left the house.

'The crows will show us,' said Sadie. 'They promised.'

'I dunno,' said Walter. 'I don't reckon the crows
are going to speak no more.'

Sadie's heart skipped. 'How come?'

'It just feels like that's all over. Since you found
Jimmy's tin and gave it to Auntie. Since we went and
saw Lachie in hospital and sorta made friends again.
I dunno.'

'But it's not finished. Auntie Lily said we had to
mark his grave, and she said we should take him back
to his own country.'

'We don't know where Jimmy's country is.'

Sadie searched her memory. 'Down south, he said. By the sea.'

Walter raised his eyebrows. 'Lots of sea out there.'

'Well, we'll have to worry about that later. Maybe the crows will tell us where he came from.'

'Gotta find his grave first,' said Walter. 'Maybe that's the end.'

Sadie didn't answer. She had a feeling that Crow's stories were sunk so deep in the bones of this country that they would never break off, never be finished. They would circle around as the stars circled, always changing, always the same. She shivered.

'You think he'll really come?' She meant Lachie.

Walter shrugged. 'He said he would.'

They walked on in silence, their shoes squelching softly in the mud.

'Look.' Sadie pointed at a thicket of dead tree trunks poking up from the sediment. 'The graveyard was practically in the bush back then.'

They halted, looking around at the flat expanse of mud. It was hard for Sadie to remember the landscape as it was before the dam choked the vegetation, drowned the buildings and swallowed up the old graves.

She stared down at the crooked crosses scattered over the ground. 'None of these are attached to their graves any more. Jimmy could be anywhere.'

'We'll never know,' said Walter.

Sadie grabbed his arm. They held their breath as a crow hopped toward them. It flapped and bowed as if it were dancing, then stopped and stared at them, as if to be sure they were watching. '*Wah!*' It jabbed with its beak. '*Wah!*'

'Here,' breathed Sadie. 'Jimmy's here.'

Walter shrugged. 'Okay.'

He slipped off his backpack and began to unload the things they'd brought: a slab of wood, a trowel, brushes and paint. 'You want to dig the hole, or paint the sign?'

'I'll paint,' said Sadie.

Walter stuck the point of the trowel into the baked ground. 'Here?' he asked the crow.

'*Wah!*' the crow agreed, and it folded its wings and watched as Walter began to dig a trough for the grave marker.

Sadie had got as far as painting *Jimmy Raven, A Clever Man*, when Walter paused and looked up. 'Here's trouble,' he said.

They both watched silently as a lanky figure moved slowly toward them across the flat plain of mud. As he came nearer, Lachie removed his hat and wiped his brow. His fair hair flopped over the bandage on his forehead.

'G'day,' he said.

Walter nodded.

The crow cried, '*Waah!*' and flapped a few paces away. It settled on the skeleton of a dead tree, where it watched them keenly.

'Not riding your bike?' said Sadie.

'Giving it a rest for a bit,' said Lachie.

'How's your head?'

Lachie fingered his bandage. 'Twelve stitches here and four in my arm,' he said with a touch of pride. 'Got the results of the scan yesterday. It's all good, they reckon.'

'Lucky. For you *and* me,' said Walter.

'Yeah.' Lachie turned his hat between his fingers. 'Thanks for, you know, getting me to the hospital and stuff.'

'Sorry about going into your house,' said Sadie. 'We shouldn't have done that. But we weren't stealing, we were trying to find some...' She hesitated. 'Some family history.'

Lachie gazed down at the scattered remains of the wooden crosses, at Sadie's half-finished marker, and Walter's half-dug hole. 'What's all this about? Some of my family's buried here, they say. Who's this Jimmy bloke? Not a Mortlock. One of your family, is it?'

'Yeah,' said Walter.

'A distant relative.' Sadie frowned, and kicked at a clod of yellow dirt. Now that the moment had come, she was finding it harder than she'd expected. 'Jimmy Raven used to work for your great-grandfather, Gerald Mortlock,' she said in a rush. 'But they had a fight, and your great-grandfather killed him. And *my* great-grandfather covered it up. He buried the body here and kept it a secret. And when Gerald made the dam, Jimmy's grave got covered up with all the other graves. And the ring of stones was covered too. It was a sacred place. That's what Jimmy and Gerald were arguing about when Jimmy was killed. Jimmy knew Gerald wanted to flood the valley, and he knew the sacred place would be destroyed. He was desperate to stop it, but Gerald wouldn't listen.'

Lachie's fists clenched and unclenched at his sides. 'You calling my great-grandpa a murderer? That's bull! He was a good man. He was a soldier in the First World War! He was a hero. We've got his medals.'

'I know,' said Sadie. 'My great-grandfather was a good man, but he did a terrible thing. Even good men make the wrong decisions sometimes.'

'I don't believe you. How do you know all this, anyway, if it was such a big secret?'

Sadie couldn't help shooting a glance at the crow on the branch, its feathers gleaming in the sun, its head cocked as it listened intently. 'A – a friend told me.'

Lachie walked away a little distance, his hands on his hips. Sadie and Walter glanced at each other. Walter wiped his mouth.

'Bethany reckons he killed himself. Our great-grandpa,' said Lachie. 'Because of the war. Post-traumatic stress or whatever. It was years after he came back. The family made out it was an accident. But Bethany thinks it was because of what he'd seen. What he'd been through.'

What he'd done, thought Sadie.

'He was shamed,' Walter said so softly that only Sadie could hear.

'All this is going to belong to me one day,' said Lachie. 'You realise that, don't you? Bethany doesn't want it. But I do. I love this place.'

'I know,' said Sadie.

Lachie twirled his hat again. He squinted at the crow. 'I had this weird dream, in hospital,' he said, almost to himself. 'Must have been the drugs…' Abruptly he crammed his hat back on his head. 'Well, if you want to put up your cross or whatever, I guess you can go ahead. Dad'll never know. He never comes here.'

Without looking at Lachie, Walter dug his trowel into the dirt. He began to whistle softly between his teeth.

'Okay,' said Sadie. 'Thanks.'

Lachie stepped closer, his hands in his pockets. He crouched, and picked up one of the fallen crosses. 'Jane Mortlock?' he read. He looked at Sadie. 'Seems a shame to leave them all lying round like this. Someone oughta tidy this place up.' He paused, then asked Walter, 'Can I borrow that, when you're finished?'

'Sure,' said Walter, without looking, intent on his digging.

Sadie dipped her brush into the paint pot and wrote: *Died 1933*.

'Looks good,' said Lachie.

'Yeah,' said Walter. 'Just needs one more thing.'

He took the brush from Sadie, and carefully painted a black feather beneath the words, like a flourish.

Together they planted the marker in the ground at the place the crow had shown them.

'I should have brought some flowers or something,' said Sadie.

'Next time,' Walter said.

'Give us a hand?' Lachie called.

The three of them moved around the tiny graveyard, straightening the fallen crosses, digging them more firmly into the ground.

'That's better,' said Lachie at last, and wiped his forehead on his sleeve. 'Maybe we should build a fence round it or something.'

'We'd help you,' said Sadie.

'Make a real headstone for Jimmy, too,' said Walter.

'Yeah,' said Lachie.

'We should try to find out more about Jimmy,' said Sadie. 'Where he came from. Then maybe one day we could take him back to his own country.'

Walter scratched his chin. 'He's been dead a long time, Sadie. How we going to do that?'

'He was a soldier in World War I. There must be records and stuff. We could look him up.'

Slowly Walter nodded. 'Yeah. Suppose we could try.'

'There's heaps of war records on the internet,' said Lachie. 'Me and Dad and Bethany looked up my great-grandpa. I could help you find Jimmy, I reckon. If you like.'

'Thanks, Lachie,' said Sadie.

'Yeah,' said Walter.

The three stood in silence, gazing at their handi-work. At last Lachie glanced at his watch. 'Better get going. The footy's starting in an hour.'

'If we can beat Wycheproof, we're into the grand final, yeah?' said Walter.

'Wycheproof's star forward's broken his leg,' said Lachie. 'So we're in with a chance.' He touched the brim of his hat. 'Well, see you round.' He began to walk away.

Sadie called out, 'Lachie!'

He turned back.

'Want to have another game of pool some time?'

Lachie flashed a brief grin. 'Sure. And bring him, will ya?' He nodded at Walter. 'I want to whip him too, while I'm at it.'

'In your dreams, mate,' called Walter.

'Yeah, we'll see who's dreaming!'

'I could beat you with one hand tied behind my back.'

'I can beat you with stitches in my arm!' yelled Lachie, pointing to his elbow.

'Yeah, right!'

'Right!'

Sadie was astonished to see the two of them grinning at each other.

Lachie gave his hat a final flourish and strode away, aiming a tremendous kick at a lump of mud. 'Goal!' he whooped, raising his arms in triumph as he received the applause of an invisible crowd, and jogged away.

'He's such a dag,' said Sadie.

'Yeah, he's all right when he's on his own,' agreed Walter. 'Want to go and see the stones?'

Sadie hesitated. 'That friend of Auntie Lily's said we shouldn't go near them till Craig builds a fence round them.'

'Just to look,' said Walter. 'Not to touch.'

'I guess,' said Sadie doubtfully.

They walked side by side across the yellow mud to the hidden dip in the ground where the stones stood in their crooked vigil. The rock that Lachie had partly dislodged had been nudged back into its former position.

'You reckon Lachie came and fixed it?' said Sadie.

'Maybe his dad?' said Walter. 'Maybe he didn't want to get into trouble with the Dja Dja Wurrung heritage guy.' He slowly circled the ring, pausing behind each silent stone. 'What did he say it might be?'

'Something to do with the stars, maybe,' said Sadie. 'Lining up with different constellations at different times of year, so they'd know the right time for ceremonies.'

Walter nodded. 'That's what the carvings are about?'

'Maybe. He's not sure.'

'Pity you can't go back a few thousand years and ask them,' said Walter. 'The people who used to live here.'

'Yeah,' said Sadie. 'Pity.'

*

The crow that had followed them across the lake bed swooped up to perch on top of one of the tall stones. It watched as the girl and the boy stood back from the sacred place, showing respect, as they should. The crow preened its feathers.

The boy straightened up. 'Better go, if we don't want to miss the footy.'

'I'll follow you in a minute,' the girl said.

The boy shrugged, hoisted his bag on his shoulder and walked away, his shadow wavering over the yellow mud and the tussocky swamp plants. The girl watched him go, then she turned to face the crow.

'Hey,' she said, in a low voice. 'I need to ask you something.' She glanced back over her shoulder, but the boy was still walking. The girl took a step closer. 'I went to the cemetery. I wanted to visit the other Sadie's grave...but it was gone.' She glanced over her shoulder again. 'Clarry's was still there, and Gerald Mortlock, and all the others, but Sadie's – it just wasn't there.'

The crow tilted its head. The girl pushed her hair behind her ears.

'So – I went home, and I asked Mum if she knew anything about my great-aunt Sadie. And she laughed at me. She said, of course she knew about her, otherwise she wouldn't have named me after her. She said Sadie was an amazing woman who travelled round the world and had all these incredible adventures and lived till she was eighty-three. And I said, I thought she died when she was fourteen. And Mum said, where did you get that idea from? And I said, I thought I was called Sadie because I was born on Saturday. And Mum looked at me as if I'd gone mental, and she said, *no!* And I checked my birth certificate, and it's true, I'm called Sadie – short for Sarah, not Saturday.'

The girl licked her lips, and glanced around again. 'So what I want to know is – did Waa change history? Did *I* change history? Did Waa – I dunno – take back Sadie's punishment, or something? Did he stop being angry with her? Is that why she lived?'

The girl stared at the crow, half-bold, half-pleading.

'*Waaah,*' said the crow. '*Waa-aaah.*'

The girl shook her head. 'I don't understand... I can't understand you any more.'

'*Waah,*' said the crow, sadly.

'Does that mean Walter's right? It really is all over?'

'*Waaaah!*'

The girl's face crinkled in frustration. 'Does that mean yes or no?'

'*Waah!*'

The girl spread her hands. 'Then I guess I'd better say goodbye.'

The crow shifted on its perch, and then it unfurled its wings and flapped lazily away, climbing into the empty sky.

Far below, Sadie flung back her head. 'Goodbye, Crow! Goodbye, Waa! Only – this is your country, isn't it? You're not going anywhere.'

And from far above her, invisible in the wide blue sky, came the distant echo of a crow's laughter.

Acknowledgements

With thanks to Gary Murray and the Dja Dja Wurrung people, for allowing me to tell this story.

Thanks to Ngarra Murray for the cover illustration; to Susannah Chambers, Eva Mills and Jodie Webster at Allen & Unwin for their unfailing help and encouragement; and to Michael, my personal First World War historian.

About the author

Kate Constable is a Melbourne writer who grew up in Papua New Guinea. She is the author of the internationally-published fantasy trilogy, *The Chanters of Tremaris*, as well as *The Taste of Lightning*. As part of the *Girlfriend* Fiction series, she has written *Always Mackenzie* and *Winter of Grace* (joint winner of the Children's Peace Literature Award, 2009) and co-authored *Dear Swoosie* (with Penni Russon). Her novel *Cicada Summer* was short-listed for the 2010 Prime Minister's Literary Award (Children's Fiction).

Kate lives in West Preston with her husband, two daughters and a bearded dragon.